She may have just met him, but the world was a better place because he existed, a safer place.

She was sure of it. Giving in to whatever that warmth moving through her was, she placed her hand on his arm, hoping he understood what she didn't know how to express given the short time since they'd met. *How had it only been days when she felt as if she'd always known him?* How was it that touching him felt so right and yet as if she should jerk away her hand before it was branded by the feel of his skin beneath her fingertips?

Seeming to pull himself from wherever his thoughts had gone, he shifted his mirrored gaze to where her fingers pressed against his arm, then lifted his eyes to hers. Ivy dropped her hand to her side. She didn't drag her gaze from where he looked at her from behind those blasted sunglasses, though. The connection was so powerful she didn't feel as if she could.

Dear Reader,

I had the privilege of volunteering for a legacy flight during the summer of '23. Meeting the WWII veterans on the trip and the people of Normandy was life-changing. With the powerful emotions evoked, it only made sense that I'd want to write a story set around the event. Only truly special characters would work, though.

Dr. Ivy McEwen had volunteered as the medic for the Smoky Mountain Veteran Foundation to honor her WWII hero great-grandfather, not to add another dating mistake to her already-long list.

After an injury ended his military career, army paratrooper Caleb Rivers found new life meaning by becoming a paramedic to help others. Filling in for his buddy's volunteer spot on a veteran legacy trip was a no-brainer. But when he meets the doctor in charge of the medical team, it's his heart on the line. He's been burned before. Can Ivy accept him as he is?

I hope you enjoy their story and the glimpses into the beauty of Normandy, France, and the very special people who live there and stole my heart.

Janice

RISKING IT ALL
WITH THE PARAMEDIC

JANICE LYNN

MEDICAL ROMANCE

MEDICAL ROMANCE

Recycling programs for this product may not exist in your area.

ISBN-13: 978-1-335-94252-4

Risking It All with the Paramedic

Harlequin Enterprises ULC
22 Adelaide St. West, 41st Floor
Toronto, Ontario M5H 4E3, Canada
www.Harlequin.com

Printed in U.S.A.

USA TODAY and Wall Street Journal bestselling author **Janice Lynn** has a master's in nursing from Vanderbilt University and works as a nurse practitioner in a family practice. She lives in the southern United States with her Prince Charming, their children, their Maltese named Halo and a lot of unnamed dust bunnies that have moved in after she started her writing career. Readers can visit Janice via her website at janicelynn.com.

Books by Janice Lynn

Harlequin Medical Romance

A Surgeon to Heal Her Heart
Heart Surgeon to Single Dad
Friend, Fling, Forever?
A Nurse to Tame the ER Doc
The Nurse's One Night to Forever
Weekend Fling with the Surgeon
Reunited with the Heart Surgeon
The Single Mom He Can't Resist
Heart Doctor's Summer Reunion
Breaking the Nurse's No-Dating Rule

Visit the Author Profile page
at Harlequin.com for more titles.

**Janice won the National Readers' Choice Award
for her first book,
The Doctor's Pregnancy Bombshell.**

To Honoring Veteran Legacies, the Best Defense
Foundation and Veterans Back to Normandy.
Thank you for all you do to honor those who served.

CHAPTER ONE

"I WAS AFRAID you'd change your mind about going."

Dr. Ivy McEwen paused from wheeling her luggage beside her at the Knoxville airport departure terminal area to smile at the seventy-year-old daughter of one of the World War II veterans she'd be with almost nonstop over the next two weeks. Ivy had changed her mind a dozen times. That had been just in the past hour. How could she be so excited to be a medical volunteer for a veteran legacy flight to Normandy, France, and so emotionally devastated at the same time?

"Gramps wanted me to go." She fought to keep her emotions checked. She'd cried enough tears the night before while inspecting her medical supplies one last time. The trip was something she had to do for the greatest man she'd ever known. She'd forever regret it if she didn't follow through on the plans they'd made prior to her great-grandfather passing two months ago.

"You're right. Leon would want you watching

out for us." Mary gave an empathetic look. "Dad and I sure feel better knowing that you'll be taking care of us."

Not that Mary knew anything about Ivy's medical skills other than what Gramps had bragged to the Smoky Mountain Veteran Foundation.

Bless him.

He'd set the bar high, but then, when hadn't he? Ivy had spent most of her life making sure she not only met but exceeded his expectations. She'd wanted to make Gramps proud. Always.

"It's an honor to be on the medical team." With D-Day having occurred on June 6, 1944, there wouldn't be many more WWII legacy trips to honor those who had helped liberate Europe.

"Speaking of the medical team…" Mary waggled her penciled-on reddish brown brows that perfectly matched her dyed hair cut in a trendy bob. "Have you met the paramedic who took Stan's place? He makes this old gal want to call 911."

Ivy appreciated Mary's subject change to lighten the conversation. She'd instantly liked the woman when they'd met months ago at one of the few planning meetings Ivy had been able to attend while she'd been finishing her medical school out-of-state residency.

"I haven't." Stan had canceled last minute due to a family emergency. Regardless, Ivy and Lara, a nurse from Maryville, should be able to handle most medical situations that might occur while traveling with five almost-centenarians. Ivy grinned at how Mary dramatically fanned her flushed cheeks. "Mary, do I need to check your blood pressure?"

Mary laughed. "Probably. He's a handsome one. Linda asked him if he was available."

"Linda isn't available," Ivy reminded of the married fifty-two-year-old granddaughter of one of the veterans.

"No, but you are." Mary waggled her brows again. "He's single and a real hottie."

"Not interested." Ivy hoped the women weren't going to play matchmaker. The only thing she could imagine worse than having to get on an airplane would be getting into a new relationship. Luke had left her with a terrible aversion to another relationship. Blech. No, thank you. "Besides, looks fade, Mary."

Grabbing hold of her suitcases' handles, Ivy rolled them toward the departure terminal counter. As much as she dreaded the flight, she needed to check in. Maybe the knot in her stomach would ease once she'd taken that step.

Mary kept pace. "True, looks fade. But some men are classically handsome throughout their lifetime. You can see their beauty no matter how much time has tried to ebb it away."

Ivy knew exactly what she meant. She'd felt it every time she'd looked at her great-grandfather.

She'd always known why her great-grandmother had been besotted with the paratrooper when he'd returned from Europe in 1945. Later in his life, Ivy had thought he'd hung the moon and soaked up every moment she got to spend with him. Why didn't they make men like Gramps anymore? Men who were honorable, brave, skilled, loyal, *faithful*, and not threatened by a woman's success? Today's men just weren't of the same caliber.

"Caleb is that kind of handsome," Mary continued as they walked toward where the others waited near the group meeting point. "Stan did us right by asking him to join us. When we got here, he jumped right in to help with our luggage. I haven't heard so many 'Yes, ma'ams' and 'No, ma'ams' as when I was talking with him. Mark my words, he's a keeper." The woman's gaze went beyond Ivy and she grinned like a Cheshire cat. "Oh! He and Owen are back from the restroom now. Have a gander, and it may be you needing to have *your* blood pressure checked."

"You're a funny lady, Mary, but I'm not interested." Three strikes and she was out. She'd thought Luke, aka Heartbreak Number Three, was different, but he'd been cheating for months with an undergrad student he'd first met at a Christmas party he'd attended with Ivy. To top it off, he'd blamed Ivy. Just recalling his unjustified attempts at shifting the blame for his unfaithfulness had her fingers curling into her palms. If he'd felt inadequate, it had been because he was. Too bad it had taken discovering he'd been sleeping with Little Miss Coed for Ivy to finally admit that she'd been blind because she'd wanted to believe in their relationship. Not so long ago, she'd dreamed of having what Gramps and her great-grandmother had had. She forced her fingers to relax their tight grasp on her luggage handle. She wasn't letting Luke, or any man, sully this trip to honor Gramps's legacy.

"You should keep an open mind," Mary sighed dreamily. "Or maybe I should say an open heart?"

"No, thank you." She'd be keeping her heart to herself.

Mary had the audacity to laugh.

That's when Ivy spotted Caleb Rivers. Although she'd never met him or even seen a photo, the man walking beside Owen had to be whom Mary went on about. She hadn't been kidding about that blood pressure check. Despite Ivy's aversion to the male species, her pulse did a wild dance, proving that she was still a young, healthy female who wasn't as oblivious as she'd like to think.

Younger than she'd been expecting as she'd imagined someone closer to Stan's age, Caleb wore his dark hair cropped short but not quite in a buzz. Long lashes fringed intense amber eyes. A slightly crooked nose hinted that it had once been broken. Rather than detract, the imperfection added to his manly appeal. He was tall, probably six-two or three and thick-chested but not in an "I'm on steroids" way. He was easy on the eyes, but ultimately what did that matter? With Ivy's dating history, good looks were a detriment as they made a man a more appealing target for other women. With as much as she'd been cheated on, maybe it really was her fault the men she dated had all betrayed her.

"Caleb." Mary waved at where he stayed close to Owen. "Come here. I want to introduce you to Dr. Ivy."

Mr. Ruggedly Handsome shifted his gaze toward Mary. Ivy's breath caught. Okay, there was something about him that turned her insides to goop.

Pheromones, Ivy. That's what's about him. Pheromones wrapped in a gorgeous package. You're used to academic types, not someone so...physical. She was over relationships, but not physically dead.

A woman might have to be dead not to notice Caleb River's manliness. An aura clung to him that assured he could take care of business, whatever that business might be, and yet, when he'd turned toward Mary, his smile was warm and genuine. Right up until his gaze met Ivy's. At that point something flickered that made her want to spin her luggage around and hightail it out of the airport. Or maybe just spontaneously combust right then and there because warm had shot to *hot*.

Not once could she recall having had such an instantaneous reaction. She'd dated Luke during residency because he'd been intelligent, attractive in a scholarly, dependable way and she'd thought they shared the same values. Luke had replaced Beau who she'd dated during medical school, but who had rekindled a relationship with his high school girlfriend during a trip home to visit his family over the Christmas holidays. Only, he'd forgotten to mention that tidbit for several months and had been stringing both women along until the girlfriend back home had gotten pregnant. Beau had replaced Kenny from undergrad. Kenny had said he loved Ivy, but she'd eventually learned that he'd "loved" lots of women. Yea, her track record wasn't so good when it came to men. Forcing herself to stand as tall as her five-six would stretch with her heavy backpack weighing her down, Ivy straightened her shoulders. Gorgeous Caleb Rivers had probably broken so many hearts he made the men of Ivy's past look like child's play.

He said something to Owen, then they crossed the twenty or so feet to her and Mary. Caleb kept his pace matched with Owen's slower, but steady one, not touching him, but aware of every nuance. Good for him for realizing that the proud veteran would have been insulted if he'd attempted to unnecessarily assist him in any way.

When they joined where Ivy and Mary had stopped just feet from the counter, Owen grinned. "Glad to see you, Doc."

"You, too." It was true. She'd fallen hard for the veterans she'd met during the information sessions she'd attended, especially Owen. There was something dapper yet tough about him. When he'd talked about his late wife, Ivy had gotten goose bumps at the love in his voice. Sometimes, she thought she'd been born in the wrong generation.

"You've not met Caleb?" Was there an extra twinkle in Owen's pale blue gaze that hinted he and Mary were on the same page? Ugh. She really hoped she wouldn't be dealing with a bunch of wannabe Cupids the entire trip.

"No, sir. I haven't." She shifted her gaze from Owen to the paramedic and swallowed. She might need to send her hormones a memo that she was not interested even if they had blossomed to unexpected life.

With a friendly smile cutting dimples into his cheeks, Caleb stuck out his hand. "Caleb Rivers. Nice to meet the infamous doctor who Owen keeps telling me about." His eyes danced with a mischievous gleam. "You have a lot to live up to, but so far, he was right on the money."

Interesting. What had Owen told Caleb? And

why were her lips curving upward in such a huge smile? Puh-leeze. Had she learned nothing? Apparently not, because when she gripped his outstretched hand, every nerve ending in her body started and ended where their skin touched.

Hello, lightning bolt.

Goodness. Obviously, her lack-of-sleep brain was playing tricks on her.

"Dr. Ivy McEwen." Determined to shake off whatever insanity was gripping her, she pulled her hand from Caleb's, marveling at how her hand threatened to rebel and return to the warm, firmness of his callused grasp. "Don't believe a thing this ancient coot tells you." She kissed Owen's cheek. "Are you ready for this?"

Owen's eyes sparkled. "I'm always ready for traveling the world with a beautiful woman." His expression turned serious. "It's been a long time since I've set foot in France."

Ivy's heart squeezed. He and Gramps had instantly clicked when they'd first met. Ivy had devoured the stories the two men had shared in between the organization's coordinator running through the proposed trip itinerary.

Owen gestured toward Caleb. Pride shone on his weathered face. "This guy was in the Eighty-Second, too, just like your great-grandfather and me."

Surprised by Owen's revelation, although not sure why since she knew very little about Stan's last-minute replacement other than a few shared group text messages and what Mary had told her, Ivy glanced toward the paramedic. Her gaze collided with his as he'd apparently been watching her rather than looking at Owen. Her breath caught. "You were a paratrooper?"

Ivy would swear he grew a few inches taller. "Yes, ma'am."

Mary nudged Ivy at his good manners, as if to say, *See what I mean?*

"Much to my mother's chagrin—" Caleb grinned "—jumping out of perfectly good airplanes is all I ever wanted to do."

She could tell it was an auto-response he must give often, because it flowed so smoothly. Yet there was something in his eyes that hinted there was more to what he was saying.

"I hear your love of jumping. But you're working as a paramedic. Should I ask why the career change?"

He shrugged. "Being a paratrooper is a job for the young."

"I've seen your trip health form. You're not that old," she pointed out, then felt her cheeks go hot. Maybe she should point out that she'd intently reviewed everyone going on the trip's forms to proactively plan for any potential issues.

Owen chuckled. "That's right. He's barely old enough to need to shave."

Ivy took in the strong lines of Caleb's jaw, surprised by how much she wanted to run her fingers across the smooth-shaven skin. She'd put money on his having shaved that morning, and it wouldn't surprise her if he had stubble prior to their reaching their host family in France. She'd never been attracted to stubble, preferring a clean-cut appearance, but she suspected that Caleb could pull off most looks.

"Just barely." Caleb chuckled at Owen's teasing, then focused on Ivy. "My career change is a long story. Let's get your bags checked."

Ivy was disappointed that he hadn't given her an answer. She had a natural curiosity about people, about all aspects of life, really. Caleb Rivers intrigued her more than most, which wasn't necessarily a good thing.

Ivy didn't need help with her two roller bags and backpack, but Luke's insults echoed about how she refused to allow a man to be a man, citing her heftier income as making her too independent. Ivy pointed to the suitcase she planned to check. "If you put that bag on the scale, you might prevent me from toppling over."

See, that hadn't been that difficult. Then again, she didn't want Luke being the voice in her head that dictated future actions.

"No toppling. You're not allowed to get hurt."

That would be a travesty since she was there to take care of others. How her heart fluttered at

Caleb's eyes crinkling in the corners was enough to have her knees buckling, though.

Cheeks warm, she pulled her gaze from him to the duo watching her curiously. "Mary, you and Owen behave while I get checked in."

With a twinkle in their eyes that suggested they might purposely seek trouble, they laughed. Mary linked her arm with Owen's and they walked to where her father and the others waited. Owen's great-granddaughter Suzie tried to get him to sit in one of the empty wheelchairs near the bench. If looks could kill, Owen would be facing time. He patted the girl's hand then, continuing to stand, started talking to a send-off volunteer.

Having watched the exchange, Caleb grabbed the handle of Ivy's largest suitcase. "He's probably hoping that thing disappears to where no one suggests he sit in it again. He sure wasn't happy about my suggestion I push him in it when he had to go to the restroom."

"None of them are going to want to use a chair any more than they absolutely have to. I'm glad. It's good for them to move as much as they can before we get on the plane. Knoxville to Paris is a long way for them to travel."

It was a long way for Ivy to travel. Logically, she knew all the reasons why flying was safer than driving, but her aerophobia was impervious to logic. Always had been.

Caleb nodded. "True. I'm going to struggle

with trying to protect them to the point of annoying them."

"No worries. They'll set you straight." She moved to the check-in point and fought nausea. Why couldn't she love flying the way her parents did? People flew all the time and were just fine. She would be, too. If the flight to Paris was too bad, she'd take a boat back to the States. Which wouldn't work since she'd never abandon the veterans in her care. One way or another, she'd endure the round-trip flights. With what the veterans had once endured, she could handle a few hours of discomfort.

Ivy gave the woman at the counter her passport and ticket information. When Caleb put her bag upon the scale, Ivy held her breath. Her bag came in just under the weight limits.

"That was close." Caleb grinned. "Does this one go?"

She shook her head. "That one stays with me. It and my backpack are full of medical supplies."

Smiling, Caleb gestured toward where the others from their group were. Amongst the various luggage items were a camouflage backpack and a sturdy black hard-case bag. "I feel ya."

Ivy's face heated. Ha! Her whole body heated. Which was ridiculous. What was wrong with her? She blamed Mary's earlier comments.

As distracting as he was, Caleb would not be "feeling her" short of her suffering a heart attack on the plane brought on by her anxiety and his needing to perform cardiopulmonary resuscitation. With the way her heart pounded, his needing to revive her might not be such a far-fetched possibility.

From where he sat across the aisle from her while they awaited their plane's turn to take off, Caleb Rivers studied the brunette bombshell whose eyes were closed. He'd heard so much about her from everyone he'd met in connection to Smoky Mountain Veteran Foundation. They all adored Dr. Ivy McEwen. Several had mentioned her beauty, including the ninety-nine-year-old veteran in the plane seat next to him. Caleb had worried that he'd be dealing with a prima donna, but was reassured that Ivy was willing to lose her personal items over her medical supplies.

The moment his gaze had connected with hers, the same headiness had rushed through him that he got when free-falling through the sky during a jump. It had been a long time, too long, since he'd experienced that sensation. From a jump or a woman. Ivy's long shiny dark hair was braided. Faint freckles kissed her lightly tanned skin across her nose and cheeks. Her lips were plump and rosy. Her eyes were what had sucker punched him, though. Big blue irises shaded by lashes so perfect he wondered if they were extensions like TransCare's receptionist wore. Ivy was a knockout, no doubt about it. That she was intelligent was a given, but something in the way she'd looked at him seemed to see beyond the surface, too.

Her eyes opened and met his. "Everything okay?"

He'd like to ask her that because of the fatigue showing on her facial features. Had she not slept well the night before? For all he knew, she'd worked and headed straight to the airport at the end of a shift.

"I'll make sure the guys get up to walk in an hour or so, if you want to grab a nap," he offered, hoping she'd feel comfortable as long as she knew their veterans were being taken care of. The foundation had purposely requested that the medical team be in aisle seats so they could more readily get to anyone who needed them. Lara was toward the front of the plane near part of their group. Near the rear, Ivy sat in the left side row, with Owen sandwiched between her and his granddaughter at the window. Caleb sat in the middle row section with Roy next to him and Mary in the opposite middle section aisle seat.

Looking alarmed, guilty almost, Ivy shook her head. "I hadn't planned to sleep."

"No?" He arched a brow. "It'll be morning in France when we arrive. We should all rest while we can."

Her fingers white-knuckled the seat belt strap.

"I'm fine. You can nap. I'm not much for sleeping on planes, but even if I was, I'm not tired." It was early morning in Tennessee, but the six-hour time difference would catch up with them at the end of their flight, especially if Ivy hadn't slept much the night before. Did she struggle just with takeoff or flying in general? Although he loved flying, he empathized with those who did not. Maybe he could distract her during takeoff enough to ease some of her anxiety.

"We've been cleared for takeoff," the captain said over the loudspeaker.

The plane moved onto the runway strip. The skin stretched across Ivy's knuckles as she gripped her seat belt strap more tightly.

Caleb fought the urge to reach across the aisle to place his hand over hers. If he could do it without being so obvious, he would. Ivy's fear was real, but he knew she fought to hide it and wouldn't appreciate his doing anything that pointed it out to others. "You've got this and you're going to be fine," he encouraged in a low voice.

Her gaze met his and she tilted her chin ever so slightly. "Residency has me well prepared to function on little to no sleep."

Stan had mentioned that she'd just finished her residency. He suspected she knew he hadn't been referring to napping, but he went with it.

"It's been a while, but the army did the same

for me." Memories assailed him, good and bad, but he forced his focus toward the good. "It also taught me to sleep whenever I got the chance, so I generally do."

She narrowed her gaze. "You're one of those annoying people who can nod off anywhere, aren't you?"

He grinned. "Guilty. How did you guess?"

"Just a hunch," she admitted, her fingers flexing, then smoothing over the seat belt strap as if she'd like to put it back in a death hold but was forcing herself not to as the plane increased in speed. Taking a deep breath, she rushed on. "That's never been me. I'm not a napper and usually don't try to sleep if I don't have at least four hours. Less than that, I feel worse than if I'd not slept at all."

He wrinkled his nose. "That must have been rough during residency. With the long hours, I'd have thought you'd sleep whenever given the chance."

"If only I had an on-off switch to make that happen. I wanted to be a doctor, so I did what I had to do regardless of how much sleep I did, or didn't, get." Another forced smile, then she failed to do anything other than hold her breath as the plane lifted off the ground. Sighing, she met his gaze with a warning in her blue depths not to point out what had just happened. Her chin was lifted in that show of defiance, causing something to stir deep within him. Empathy, he assured himself. No one liked seeing someone else suffer and takeoff had certainly not been a pleasurable experience for Ivy.

"What made you want to be a doctor?"

She took a deep breath, as if she really didn't want to be talking but to focus on what was happening to the plane.

"My great-grandmother was a doctor." She glanced toward the window two seats from her. "She was a pioneer, since at the time most physicians were male. She died when I was young, unfortunately. Gramps told me stories about her and how she loved taking care of others. I wanted to honor her legacy."

"And ended up in Knoxville?"

"Gramps's farm is just outside Knoxville, so Knoxville has always felt like home." She grimaced, her face going pale, then corrected herself. "He passed a couple of months ago."

"I'm sorry," Caleb said. He'd been told that, originally, she'd been going on this trip to accompany her great-grandfather, who had served in World War II.

"Me, too." She gave a tight smile, then obviously unable to keep her hands still, she tightened her seat belt again. "You should get one of those power naps you were bragging about while you have the chance."

Rather than continue their conversation, Ivy

turned from him, saying something to Owen, which the natural-born talker jumped all over. Caleb wasn't used to being dismissed but that was what she'd done. The opposite sex usually found him attractive. He'd taken advantage of that to the fullest in his younger years until he and Katrina had started dating, but since his accident he hadn't had time for frivolous encounters and wasn't interested in anything more. Maybe his reaction to Ivy was his body's way of telling him he'd been on hiatus too long.

Even without Katrina's rejection of his life choices, women hadn't been a priority. Healing his ankle had consumed him. He'd moved on, had a different life now. It wasn't the one he'd planned on, but he liked to think he still made a difference in the world even if those closest to him didn't agree with his choices.

Frustrated by his own limitations, he stretched out the best his economy seat would allow while keeping his feet out of the aisle so he wouldn't trip anyone. Maybe he'd get lucky, doze off for a while, and, hopefully, not dream of the life-altering event that had robbed him of his greatest joy.

Otherwise, it might be Ivy having to reach across the airplane aisle to calm him.

CHAPTER TWO

HAVING TRULY DOZED off and fortunately not experiencing any nightmares, Caleb awakened when about an hour into the flight a stewardess came over the public address system.

"Are there any medical personnel on the plane?" she asked. "Would any medical personnel on board please come to the back of the plane? Thank you."

Coming fully alert, Caleb unsnapped his seat belt. When he stepped into the aisle, Ivy was already out of her seat and headed to the back.

"You're medical?" a stewardess asked as they reached the back of the plane.

"I'm Dr. McEwen and Mr. Rivers is a paramedic," Ivy informed the woman, whose face immediately filled with relief.

"Great. A passenger isn't feeling well and is having trouble breathing. Come this way."

A flush-cheeked female in her late forties hunched on the other side of the back galley. Several people crowded around her. With her expression panicked and tears flowing, she shook her head at whatever someone had asked her.

"Step back," the stewardess told the other airline employees and the man huddled around the distressed woman. "This is a doctor."

All except the man who had his arm on her shoulder, perhaps the woman's husband, stepped back, giving a grateful look toward Caleb and Ivy.

"Hello, I'm Dr. McEwen." Ivy stepped forward. "Is it okay for me and my paramedic acquaintance, Caleb, to examine you?" The woman nodded and Ivy asked, "What's your name?"

"Bella…" The woman's name came out with a bit of a croaking sound. The woman coughed to try to clear her throat. Her scared gaze cut to her husband, obviously pleading with him to do something.

"So that I can best help you, tell me what's going on, Bella." Ivy refocused the woman's attention on her.

"I…can't…breathe," she managed, sounding more and more hoarse. She glanced toward the man with her, again, and he took over speaking for her.

"I'm Bella's husband, Tom," he said. "We were sitting in our seats, and she started feeling funny, saying she felt tingly and itchy. Then she started breathing funny. We weren't sure what to do so I pressed the stewardess button. They had us come to the back of the plane."

"That was the right thing to do," Caleb assured while Ivy stayed focused on the woman. He reached for Bella's wrist. Her rapid pulse bounded beneath her clammy skin. Glancing at his watch, he counted for fifteen seconds, then multiplied the number by four. "Tachycardic at 120."

"Bella, I'd like you to open your mouth as wide as you can and stick out your tongue," Ivy advised as she turned on her phone's flashlight and shined it into the woman's mouth. She didn't grimace exactly, but Caleb could tell Ivy didn't like what she saw. "Your throat is swollen. Are you allergic to anything? Peanuts, maybe? If so, do you have an epinephrine pen to counter the reaction?"

Looking more and more panicked, Bella shook her head.

"She's not allergic to anything," Tom assured them. "No medications, foods, nothing."

"She's allergic to something and is having an anaphylactic reaction." Ivy turned toward Caleb. "I have an epinephrine injection pen in my backpack. Go get my entire bag, please, and bring it here."

Although his instinct was to stay with the patient, Caleb immediately fast-walked across the crew area then back up the aisle to where Ivy's backpack was stored beneath the seat in front of hers. Grabbing it and his own bag from the overhead bin, he returned to the back section of the plane as quickly as he safely could.

Bella was now sitting on the floor and was actively wheezing and holding her chest. Ivy knelt beside her and was reassuring her that she had the appropriate medications to stop the reaction. Ivy held Bella's wrist, no doubt keeping a check on her pulse. The poor woman's husband looked a mess and one of the flight attendants, appearing almost as harried, was on the phone with the pilot, advising him of what was happening.

"The doctor says we have to land the plane," the stewardess was saying into the phone.

Caleb agreed. The sooner, the better.

"Thank you." Ivy took her bag, unzipped it and pulled out a pouch where she quickly found what she was looking for.

Kneeling beside them, Caleb opened his own bag and found his pulse oximeter. He slipped the oxygen saturation monitor over the woman's fingertip. "Eighty-nine percent oxygen saturation and a 128 heart rate." He glanced toward another of the stewardesses. She held a pen and paper and was making notes. "It's probably what you're doing, but, if not, I'd appreciate you writing down vital signs, along with the time, as Dr. McEwen or I say them. Same goes with medications given. That way we can reference them if needed. Thanks."

The stewardess nodded. "Got it. I have to keep a record of what happens anyway for our report."

While Ivy jabbed the epinephrine pen into the woman's thigh, releasing the medication, Caleb reached for his blood pressure cuff to get diastolic and systolic readings.

"Bella, this was epinephrine." The woman barely reacted to the injection and seemed oblivious to where Caleb was wrapping the cuff around her arm. Her gaze jumped back and forth between Ivy and her husband. "It's a medication to help with your allergic reaction. It's what you'd be given if you were at a hospital emergency department," Ivy continued, her voice calm, steady, confident. "Initially, it's probably going to make you feel shakier, sort of like you are overcaffeinated, but that's okay. It means the medicine is taking effect."

Still clutching at her chest, Bella nodded. She coughed in between her ragged, wheezy breaths. Her face had a purplish hue, appearing slick with sweat and tears and now having raised red whelps.

"The epinephrine should start taking effect quickly, but I'm going to give you an injection of diphenhydramine, too, since I have it and I only had the one epinephrine pen to give you. That should be enough, but we're on a plane, so it's better to be overly cautious." Ivy looked directly into the woman's eyes. "Diphenhydramine is something you may have taken in the past. It's over-the-counter for allergies in a capsule or tablet form as it's a common antihistamine that's been around for many decades. I'm doing the injection because I don't think you could swallow a pill right now."

"Couldn't," the woman choked out between trying to clear her throat with another wheezy cough.

Taking his stethoscope from his bag, Caleb completely agreed with Ivy's decision process and admired how she worked efficiently while trying to keep Bella calm and focused on her. At over thirty thousand feet in the air, they needed to hit Bella with everything they could to get her reaction under control. While Ivy dug through the medication vials in the pouch she'd pulled the epinephrine injectable pen from, he paused in taking Bella's blood pressure and instead reached into Ivy's bag for the plastic packet stuffed with syringes and needles. He got out one of each, along with an alcohol pad, and handed them to Ivy just as she found the vial she sought.

Ivy took them. "Thanks."

While she drew up the diphenhydramine, he finished taking Bella's blood pressure.

"Eighty-four over sixty-two," he said out loud for Ivy's benefit and so the stewardess could record it. He glanced down at the pulse oximeter.

"Pulse is 134. Oxygen saturation is at 87 percent."

"Is that good or bad?" Bella's husband, Tom, asked. "The medicine is going to help, right?"

"Her blood pressure is low." The decreased pressure was from her anaphylactic shock. The epinephrine Ivy had given the woman should cause the vessels to vasoconstrict to increase the pressure quickly, though. The sooner the better. Hopefully, the medication had been given in time to prevent fluid from leaking into Bella's lungs from the reduced blood flow pressure. He didn't know what all Ivy had in her bag, but dealing with pulmonary edema on the plane would be challenging under the best of circumstances. Too bad Ivy didn't have IV supplies in her medical bag. Pumping fluids into Bella would be helpful to quickly increase her plasma volume.

"Low?" Frowning, Tom's expression grew more panicked. "Her blood pressure is usually too high. Why is it low? Is she dying?"

"No," Caleb said with great force, hoping he told the truth. With the epinephrine, he hopefully did. Either way, the last thing anyone needed was full-blown panic setting in.

"She normally has elevated blood pressure?" Ivy asked, then to Bella, "I'm going to put this injection into your hip. It's the diphenhydramine I told you about." Ivy moved to where she could readily pull the woman's elastic banded pants down to expose where she wanted to put the medication.

"Well, she used to but not recently." Tom cringed as Ivy administered the shot. "She takes blood pressure medicine. It usually works well, but not like this. She's never had a pressure this low."

"It's the release of so much histamine that's causing her blood vessels to dilate and drop her blood pressure," Ivy explained from where she was pushing the safety device on the used needle into place to prevent an accidental stick. When done, she handed it to Caleb to do something with and went back to digging through her bag. "The medication I just injected into her should counter the release of more histamine. That and the epinephrine should have you breathing easier soon, Bella."

"I hope so." Tom was starting to look a little pale himself to where Caleb worried the man might be going to pass out. They didn't need him doing so, possibly hurting himself in the process.

"Hey, Tom," he said loud enough to get the man's immediate attention. "What's the name of Bella's blood pressure medication? Is she on anything else? Prescription or over-the-counter?"

Tom took a deep breath. "I have a list of her medications in her bag that's at our seats. She has thyroid disease and takes a few vitamins, too."

"Get them," Caleb ordered. "I'd like to see her entire list."

Bella reached for her husband's hand, clutching it to her and not wanting him to go.

"I'll be right back." He pulled free to head toward their seats to fetch the list.

Glad Tom was not on a rapid descent to the plane's cabin floor, Caleb glanced at the pulse oximeter reading on Bella's finger. Her oxygen saturation was at 84 percent. She was dropping. Not good. Her tissue wasn't being properly perfused with oxygen. They needed the epinephrine and diphenhydramine to reverse her reaction fast. They also needed to get her feet elevated to help with blood flow to vital organs. Gently, so as not to topple her over, he lifted her feet, then motioned to one of the stewardesses. "I need you to hold them or for you to get me something to prop up her feet so I don't have to hold them. I need my hands free." He didn't say in case he needed to do CPR, but the thought sure rang loudly through his head.

The flight attendant took over holding Bella's feet and another went to see what she could find to keep them elevated. Ivy was still digging through her medication vials, glancing at each one, then quickly moving to the next. "I have dexamethasone with me."

Great. The steroid would help with the reaction, too.

Bella's breathing was coming hard, fast and ragged with audible wheezing.

"Bella, look at me." Caleb noted how her heart rate had spiked even higher. The woman's mascara-streaked eyes shifted to him. "It's going to be okay. Dr. McEwen and I are going to take care of you. Dr. McEwen had the right medications to give you and you got care much quicker than you would have at most places even if you'd been on the ground, rather than on a plane. Thanks to Dr. McEwen having what you needed, you're going to be okay."

What he said was true. Not that what was happening with Bella wasn't serious and even life-threatening. But with as quickly as Ivy had gotten the epinephrine into her and then the diphenhydramine, his gut instinct was that the woman was going to be okay once the medications started fully kicking in and the plane landed so they could hand her over to ground emergency services. Just so long as fluid hadn't leaked into her lungs. He wasn't going to go there. Only a minute or two had passed from their becoming aware of the incident, but every second was vital during a medical emergency.

Ivy pulled out the vial of dexamethasone. Swiping the top with an alcohol pad, she filled a syringe. "Sorry, Bella. I have another injection.

This one is a steroid. It'll help stop the inflammatory process and open your airway so you can breathe easier." Ivy glanced at the attendant holding Bella's feet. "I need the plane's medical box so I can see what's there. Sometimes there's IV fluid on transoceanic flights. Let's hope this is one of those times."

Another stewardess moved to the compartment above the last set of plane seats and retrieved a medical kit. She handed the bag to him. He set it on the floor, intending to go through it, but Ivy immediately undid the fastener and began searching through the bag. She outranked him, so he didn't resent her take-charge attitude. If anything, he liked it.

"Yes! This may come in handy." Excited, she picked up a vial of epinephrine and showed it to him. Good. They had backup adrenaline.

Pulling a five-hundred-milliliter bag of normal saline from the kit and supplies to start an IV, Ivy smiled. "Now, we're in business."

As a paramedic, Caleb dealt with life-threatening situations on a regular basis. Enough so that he wasn't even sure his own adrenaline got up much these days when working a call. However, Dr. Ivy McEwen's smile had just gut punched him with a dose so huge his breath caught, and he almost felt dizzy from its impact.

The next two weeks were going to be interesting to say the least.

* * *

Ivy double-checked that she had everything she needed within reach so she could start Bella's IV. *Saline bag, tourniquet, antiseptic, insertion catheter, tubing, gauze, tape, gloves*, she mentally ticked the items off.

She quickly swabbed her hands again with a disinfectant packet, then gloved up, opened the packaging around the bag of saline, attached the tubing and filled the line with fluid, making sure she'd cleared out air bubbles.

"I'll hold it," Caleb offered, jumping to his feet and taking the bag from her. "Or if you want me to start the line, I'll do that. Either way, I'm good."

"I've got it," she assured. She hoped she told the truth. She was usually a great stick, but she'd never started an IV on a plane at over thirty thousand feet.

Lord, please don't let them hit any turbulence.

She put the tourniquet on Bella's arm and cleansed her antecubital space, trying not to wince at what she felt. Bella wasn't going to be an easy stick.

"This is going to be interesting," she mumbled under her breath as she opened the catheter. "Keep your fingers crossed," she told no one in particular as she readied the catheter, then slid it into the woman's vein. Holding her breath, she released the tourniquet and was thankful blood

filled the clear cylinder chamber. She sighed a relieved breath that she'd gotten the needle into the
vein on the first try. After feeling Bella's weak
veins, she'd definitely had her doubts that was
going to happen. "Thank you, Jesus."

She slid the catheter forward, but not the needle. Once she was happy with placement, she
removed the needle, leaving the catheter, then attached the end of the tubing Caleb held out to her.
Checking to make sure it looked right, she taped
it down to prevent the catheter from slipping out
of place. She watched closely to make sure the
fluid went into the vein and not the surrounding
tissue, and then she undid the lock mechanism
and let the fluid go at wide open.

"Nicely done," Caleb praised from where he
handed off the IV bag to a flight attendant and
moved next to Ivy. He reached for his blood pressure cuff to check the woman's vitals on her free
arm again.

"Here's her list. I had trouble finding where
she had put it, but I finally did." Tom held out a
piece of paper. Taking in that his wife now had an
IV going, his eyes widened. "What's happened?
You said she was going to be okay. Is she worse?"

"No, she's not worse," Ivy assured. "Look, the
rash on her arms is already slightly improved."
Not from the IV fluid, but from the epinephrine, diphenhydramine and dexamethasone. "She

should be breathing a little easier and continue to improve as the medication continues to work."

Bella's still frightened gaze went from watching what Caleb was doing to looking up at her husband. She motioned for Tom to sit down next to her, and he did so and clasped her hand in his.

"Her pressure is starting to come up a little already. She's ninety-four over sixty-eight," Caleb told her. "Oxygen saturation is at eighty-six. Pulse is 122."

"Her pressure and O2 sats should continue to improve." Ivy hoped. If too much fluid had leaked into Bella's lungs from the histamine reaction, getting her oxygen saturation back to normal on the plane might prove impossible. And fatal.

Over the next couple of minutes, they continued to check Bella, looking in her mouth to monitor her airway, listening to her lungs and heart, and keeping a check on her vital signs. Other than her wheeze, which didn't sound nearly as noisy as it had initially, Bella's lungs remained clear other than the sob she couldn't seem to control every few breaths. No doubt she was terrified and understandably so.

"I know it's scary, but just know the medicine is working." Ivy patted her hand. "Look at your arms. The red splotches are fading. The medicine is going to keep you feeling antsy, but you are improving. As scary as it is to feel jittery after having a reaction, that nervousness is expected from the treatment and the stress of what you've been through. You are getting better, Bella. Whether you feel it yet or not, I can see it. You are going to be okay."

If Ivy said it enough, it would hold true, right? As long as fluid hadn't leaked into Bella's lungs, everything would be fine. If it had, well, it was going to take more than what Ivy had access to on an airplane to clear the woman's symptoms. Bella would drown on her own body fluids and there wouldn't be a thing Ivy would be able to do to stop it from happening. She didn't think that was going to happen. They'd gotten to Bella quickly, given the epinephrine and other medications in time.

Hopefully.

Kneeling next to his wife, Tom made an appreciative sound.

"Take slow, deep breaths through your nose and blow them out of your mouth. Slow and steady," Caleb encouraged, keeping a close check on the pulse oximeter readings. He'd done a great job keeping a check on Bella's stats while Ivy administered medications. He'd talked with Bella and Tom with admirable kindness and compassion that seemed to make up who he was since he'd interacted with the veterans and their families in a similar manner. "Inhale through your nose," he repeated, his voice calming, a little mesmerizing even. "And blow out slowly through your mouth."

Ivy automatically fell into the breathing pattern of his words and felt some of her own tensions ease. Realizing what she'd done, she almost smiled. What a blessing he must be to his patients.

Sniffling, Bella did as Caleb said. Her breathing was still noisy, but there was an audible improvement in air movement. Excitement that what they were doing was working had Ivy doing a mental fist pump and thinking, *Yes!*

"You're doing great," Caleb encouraged in a tone that had Ivy thinking she might nickname him the Breathing Whisperer, as she was pretty sure everyone in the back galley was now breathing in sync. "Again, breathe in through your nose and now, out through your mouth. Good job, Bella. Your vital readings are looking better and better."

The stewardess who was recording the incident had been on the phone several times during the episode and currently was again. "I'll let the captain know she's improving. He wants to know what we need to do. Do we need to divert our landing still? Or can we keep going?"

Making sure she left no doubt of the seriousness of what happened to Bella, Ivy looked directly at the stewardess and said in no uncertain terms, "We have a medical emergency. Bella should be fine, but we need to get her on the ground as soon as possible so she can get continued care. We need to land."

Holding the phone to one ear, the attendant kept her gaze on Ivy. "Even though she's getting better?"

"Yes, the medications are taking effect, but we aren't crossing the ocean with someone who is having an anaphylactic reaction." She didn't want to further upset Bella or her husband, but she wasn't going to make light of what had happened. Bella could have died. She still could. "We don't know what triggered the reaction, what's going to happen when the medications start wearing off, if the worst has passed or if she'll start swelling again. We need to land. The sooner Bella gets out of this confined environment that might be providing her trigger, the better. We have to land."

The flight attendant glanced to Caleb for confirmation. Ivy fought saying something. A plane making an emergency landing was a costly big deal, and not taking anything away from Caleb, because she appreciated his help, but did the woman not think Ivy's opinion was enough?

"The pilot needs to land the plane," Caleb agreed. Perhaps sensing Ivy's irk, he added, "Dr. McEwen's quick actions and medications saved Bella's life. We're all lucky that she was here and got Bella appropriate care so quickly. But she's right in that we don't know what's going to happen when the medications wear off and whatever triggered Bella's reaction may still be a threat. Dr. McEwen knows what's best for her patient. We need to land the plane."

Warmth at his easy praise spread through her. Luke would never have made it about her but would have puffed out his chest and come up with some slightly different recommendation to elevate himself while punching holes in what she'd said. For the longest time she'd not acknowledged that was what he would do, and she'd let him mentally beat her down without her even realizing. Never again. If she ever dated again, it would only be with someone who was her superior, who wouldn't feel the need to belittle her emotionally and mentally.

"Okay," the stewardess replied, then relayed the message to the captain on the other end of the phone line.

Ivy met Caleb's gaze and although she didn't say the words out loud, she knew her face expressed her gratitude, because he gave a slight nod of acknowledgment. Maybe her surprise had showed, because his eyes held a curiosity that she didn't have time to dissect now, but suspected she would later. He was definitely what she'd label as a "manly man," and yet, he'd readily let her take control of the emergency and praised her efforts without any attempts to minimize what she'd done. That might be his most attractive quality yet and that was saying something because Mary had been right in calling him a "hottie."

Taking a deep breath, she ran her gaze over Bella again, letting everything register: her pallor, her breathing pattern, her fading rash and the pulse oximeter reading on her fingertip. "How are you feeling? Breathing any easier yet?"

"Maybe." Her voice was still hoarse and crackled with the word but was more readily understood than previous speaking efforts.

She definitely was. Her wheeze had significantly calmed. Maybe, just maybe, the worst had passed. It sure seemed that way, but Ivy knew better than to get ahead of herself when it came to the human body. Anything could happen and often did.

The pilot came over the PA system to let them know that the plane would be making an emergency landing in about twenty minutes.

Even as her stomach clenched at the thought of landing, Ivy let out a sigh of relief. Now was not the time for her aerophobia. She'd be fine.

"Did you hear that, Bella? We'll be landing soon."

"We have to have you in seats with your belts on," the stewardess told them. "For landing, we all have to be buckled in. No exceptions."

Ivy got that. She wanted that. Ivy turned to an attendant. "Can you clear out the back seats to let us sit there? I'm going to want to be close until we have her safely off the plane just in case anything changes."

The stewardess nodded and moved to talk to the passengers in the back row, then returned. "The flight is full, so they're moving to sit in your vacated seats until we're landed."

"Perfect." She glanced at Caleb. "Let's get her moved to the seat. I'd like her in the middle of us. Tom, we want you close, too."

They got situated into the back row, with Ivy taking the window seat, Bella in the middle and Caleb to the aisle. The stewardess had a passenger trade so Tom sat at the end of the aisle across from Caleb's seat. Eventually, the pilot came over the PA system to let them know that the plane was making its final descent.

Even as her stomach clenched at the thought of landing, Ivy let out a sigh of relief. "Did you hear that, Bella? We'll be on the ground soon."

Ivy's throat tightened as the words left her mouth. Now was not the time for her aerophobia. She'd be fine. Maybe.

Bella had drastically improved as her hives were almost gone and her wheeze had greatly subsided to where Ivy could only hear it when she held her stethoscope to Bella's chest. That was good, but with her patient's situation less urgent and landing imminent, moisture dampened Ivy's nape as her own fears took hold.

Her stomach roiled as the plane got lower and

lower. Now was not the time to get all panicky. Bella needed her and she sure didn't want Caleb seeing her have a meltdown over the plane landing. She'd managed during takeoff. She'd deal with landing, too. Those were always the worst parts for her, but she'd manage.

Fortunately, Tom asked Caleb something, so he turned his head toward the man, answering his question. Ivy spoke to Bella, hoping to reassure any concerns the woman might have and to distract herself with her patient, who seemed over the worst of her reaction. Thank God.

Ivy used every mental game she'd ever learned to distract herself as the plane touched ground, then roared down the runway, slowing to a stop. As soon as they'd come to a stop, they moved Bella to the back of the plane to get her ready to be transported.

Within minutes, the ground paramedics were onboard. Ivy and Caleb handed off Bella's care to them, assisting as they moved the woman off the plane. Tom followed closely with their carry-on items.

After Bella left, Ivy let out a sigh and silently told her body that it was okay, the plane was on the ground, and there was no longer need for alarm.

"Great job," a flight attendant told her, then smiled at Caleb. "Both of you were wonderful.

We were all so glad you were on the flight. Thank you so much."

"You're welcome." Ivy was a little embarrassed at the woman's gushing.

She and Caleb made their way to their seats and Ivy's embarrassment grew when the passengers clapped as they made their way through the aisle.

"You're a hero," Caleb said from behind her, causing Ivy to turn to frown. He knew they'd only been doing what they were trained to do. Nothing heroic about that. Not really.

She paused at where she'd been sitting as Lara stood from Ivy's seat.

"I went to the back of the plane to see if I could help, but you and Caleb had things under control. I'd have been in the way," the young nurse explained. "So, I stayed here to make sure these guys didn't make trouble while you and Caleb were occupied. I figured I had a better view of all our guys from back here than up where I had been sitting with the others. Oh, and, Caleb—" she looked past Ivy at where Caleb stood behind her "—Roy wanted to sit by Owen. Hope it was okay that I told him I didn't think you'd mind swapping seats. Those two have been talking nonstop. Well, mostly Owen has been talking nonstop and Roy has been listening."

"No problem," he assured.

Maybe not for him, but that meant Caleb would

now be in the middle seat of Ivy's row. Maybe Roy had just meant temporarily during the chaos, and he'd want to swap back for the actual flight. Not that Ivy minded sitting by Caleb. He seemed like a nice guy. Just…just, sitting next to Roy felt safer. Which was silly. Caleb hadn't done anything to make her feel threatened. Well, other than be in the running for Sexiest Man Alive, and on that, he unnerved her a bit.

Rather than have Caleb take the middle seat, Ivy took pity on him and his long legs. "Do you want the aisle?"

He grinned. "If you're willing, that would be great."

If there were additional emergencies on the plane, Caleb would be jumping to action as well so the few seconds lost by sitting in the middle seat shouldn't slow things much. Hopefully, they wouldn't have any other emergencies. Or be on the ground too long. Because the longer they sat, the longer she had to anticipate takeoff.

Reaching into the seat pocket in front of Caleb, she pulled out her phone, turned it off airplane mode and scrolled through messages, struggling to focus on any of them. She answered a message from her best friend, letting Jenna know that they'd had a detour but should be back in the air soon. She started to mention Caleb but didn't since she didn't want to field the questions her bestie was sure to ask.

Ivy couldn't say she was disappointed when the pilot came over the intercom to say they'd be on the ground a couple of hours to refuel and then to get worked into the takeoff schedule. The delay meant that much longer before she'd have to deal with that horrific tightness in her chest.

"You okay?" Caleb asked from next to her. He'd pulled out a book—a book she recognized as one she'd been wanting to read—and she'd thought he was engrossed in the pages. Instead, he was watching her. Perhaps in a fight-or-flight response to his presence as much as her fear of flying, she needed to move.

"We should get these guys up and moving while we don't have to worry about turbulence. We're going to have a few extra hours onboard and can't have any of them getting a blood clot. Can I get out?"

Sliding his book into the seat pocket, Caleb stood, and she jumped up, then smiled brightly at Owen sitting on the opposite aisle where Caleb had previously sat. "Come on, Owen. You and I are going for a stroll. Gotta get your blood flowing and keep those joints from getting stiff. You've got a lot of walking to do the next couple of weeks."

Owen stretched, then stood to walk around the seats. Caleb joined with Roy. Soon, most of the group fell in, looping around the middle seat section.

"We're conga dancers." Owen gestured to where the line curved around behind them.

Hearing him, Caleb began to sing an old Gloria Estefan tune.

Ivy glanced back to see him gently touching Roy's waist and dancing to the beat in conga line fashion. Something inside her eased and wound tight all at once. No. No. No. Just because he'd come across as pretty much perfect so far, he wasn't. He definitely didn't meet her criteria of making more than she did. It wasn't that she cared about the money. It was that she couldn't bear another man in her life who might feel the need to tear her down. Caleb was Heartbreak Number Four waiting to happen. She needed to steer clear.

His gaze met hers and he grinned and she felt herself weakening.

Think Luke.

"Come on, Ivy. Roy and I are showing you and Owen up back here," Caleb teased. "Come on, shake your body, baby, do the conga."

Owen chuckled, swaying his shoulders a little. "Can't have them showing us up. My dance partner is way prettier than his."

Ivy gently nudged Owen. "Ha! You just be careful you don't fall, Mr. Ninety-Eight-Years-Old-and-Dancing-in-an-Airplane-Aisle. No face-planting allowed on this trip."

The older man just laughed and waved one

arm, then the other, as he continued to slowly move forward. Although not fluid, his movements did stay with the beat. She couldn't help but smile. She loved his generation.

From behind her, Roy poked her ribs. "Do the conga."

"Why not?"

Meet a man who has me all a flutter. Save a life. Practically have a panic attack over the plane landing. Dance in the aisles. Makes sense to me. Ivy joined in their very slow conga dance, telling herself that if nothing else it gave her a good reason to hold on to Owen. She wasn't surprised when a few more passengers joined in their circle around the middle seats, and they were soon curving around from one side of the plane's aisles to the other. Younger folks danced in place while older folks inched forward while participating with a smile. Even the flight attendants who'd propped Bella's legs joined them. Several were singing along with Caleb to the lively tune.

When they'd gotten the guys back to their seats and everyone was settled to wait for the captain to let them know when they'd be able to take off again, Caleb said, "You've got to admit, so far this trip hasn't been dull."

"When it comes to being a medical volunteer, there's something to be said for dull," she reminded, causing him to chuckle. The truth was, in the cramped airplane seats, he was way too close to her for anything to feel dull. His arm brushed against hers and her stomach dived as if they were back in the air and had dropped a few thousand feet at once. She repositioned, trying to safely tuck her arm out of reach, but that was pretty much impossible in the limited space. How was she supposed to keep from accidentally touching him during the flight to Paris? What did it matter? Accidental touches were just a part of sitting next to someone on a plane, right? But that brush of his arm had been an electric jolt to her system. Ugh. So he was a gorgeous man with an overabundance of pheromones and her young, healthy body was responding to all that attractiveness. She was just human, after all. She really didn't like that she found him physically attractive, but that was life and didn't mean anything. She scooted over the remaining inch of her seat toward where Mary had put on headphones and was watching a movie. Any further and she'd be in the older woman's lap. "This 'dull' start makes me nervous about what's in store for the rest of the trip."

"Whatever happens won't be anything you can't handle." His tone was confident, full of flattery, but not facetiously so.

Turning, Ivy met his gaze. Her breath caught at the light there. Or maybe it was more at the heat that flashed through her insides at seeing desire.

He didn't bother trying to conceal his interest, but instead seemed okay with revealing that he was attracted to her.

Uh-oh. Her finding him attractive was one thing. His returning that attraction, another completely, and had her wondering if he was wrong, that she might not be able to handle everything in store during the remainder of this trip.

CHAPTER THREE

Dr. Ivy McEwen was a fascinating woman. She was also not easy to figure out. Get her to talking about something that interested her and her entire persona sparkled, but afterward she'd rein in her excitement and go back to being überprofessional.

For someone who'd just finished the long hours of residency, she had a great knowledge of the Tennessee Volunteers sport's program. Despite living in Knoxville, he was an Alabama fan.

"How is it that you know so much about local sports when you've been bogged down with residency in another state?"

"People keep up with things that are important to them, no matter how busy they are."

He arched a brow. "The University of Tennessee football team is important to you, even during offseason?"

Her gaze lowered a moment, staring at the seat back in front of her, then she shrugged. "I bleed orange 365 days a year."

"So, you get a day off every four years to roll with the tide?" he teased, referencing leap year and his favorite home state team.

She glared. "If I were you, I wouldn't count on me sporting any team color other than orange regardless of the day."

"A shame. You'd look great in black-and-white houndstooth with a big *A* across your chest."

Her gaze met and searched his. He could see she was trying to read him, trying to decipher if he was flirting or just being friendly. Both, he realized. He liked Ivy. Despite his family wishing otherwise, he wasn't in the market for a relationship, but maybe meeting Ivy would be an added bonus of the trip.

The pilot came over the loudspeaker. "Folks, I've turned the seat belt sign back on. You'll be happy to know we've been cleared for takeoff. Crew, ready the cabin."

Ivy sucked in a deep breath, then checked her already tightened seat belt. Rather than letting go of the clasp, her fingers white-knuckled the metal as if trying to make sure it stayed attached.

Caleb made sure his own seat belt was securely fastened. "I take it you're not much for flying?"

She didn't meet his gaze. "It's not my favorite thing."

"Bad experience or lifelong?"

She didn't hesitate. "Lifelong. I can't recall a time where I didn't dread flying. I hated it so much that when my parents traveled, they would drop me off to my grandparents'. Mom and Dad were schoolteachers—professors at a university in Nashville—and they spent their summers exploring the world."

Unlike his family who worked 24/7 and thought the world revolved around the almighty dollar. He supposed it could be argued that in some ways it did, but life was short and, beyond basic necessities, Caleb didn't get caught up in the things they did.

"Sounds exciting. You didn't want to go with them?"

"Not if it meant being in an airplane, but even beyond that, I'd rather have been with my grandparents." The plane started moving, slowly taxiing away from the gate where they'd been for several hours. "I know I should be glad that we're on the move, but..."

"But you're not because you like being stuck in a plane next to me? Understandable," he teased, waggling his brows. "I get that reaction all the time."

"Since you put it that way, maybe takeoff won't be so bad." Her gaze shifted to his and despite her anxiety, she half smiled. "But seriously, thanks for not making fun of me and making me feel worse than I already do that I can't conquer this silliness. I've even tried hypnosis. Nothing has helped, unfortunately."

"No reason to feel bad, Ivy. A fear of flying is common, so it's not as if you're being irrational." Rather than look reassured, her eyes squeezed shut, her long lashes peeking out from where her face squished together. A longing to trace his fingers across her face to smooth the tense lines hit so strongly that he curled his fingers into his palms. "Tell me how I can help."

Her expression remained tense. "Pray."

"Asking for divine intervention, eh? Not sure how much sway I have with the Big Guy." Probably not much. Otherwise, Blake wouldn't have died and Caleb's ankle would have healed to where he could jump again. "I'll do my best, though. Anything else?"

Both her hands now gripping her seat belt, she shook her head. "Quit talking." She sucked in a deep breath. "No, talk because I want you praying. Just, I can't have you distracting me from my misery."

He chuckled. "You're a funny lady, Ivy."

Her eyes were clenched so tightly that her cheeks practically met her eyebrows. "Good to know that if medicine doesn't work out that I have a backup career in stand-up comedy."

Wishing he could ease her discomfort, Caleb studied her profile. She really was stunning, but it was the excitement of being near her, of talking to her and hearing what would come out of her brilliant mouth next that intrigued him the most. From the moment Stan had asked him to go in his place, Caleb had known this was going to be a great trip. Meeting Ivy had certainly upped the ante.

"Medicine will work out for you."

Her eyes opened. Curiosity shined in their blue depths. "You know that after seeing me work a single patient? Maybe I was just having a good day."

"I stand by my initial assessment." Why did he get the feeling there was more to her question? That she was testing him? As if she expected him to say something that would undermine what she'd done? "You handled yourself well, with confidence, and skill," he pointed out. "Your competency and calmness saved Bella's life."

Pink tinging her cheeks, she shrugged as if his words were no big deal. He wasn't buying it. That he'd complimented her skills pleased her. He was sure of it. Her reaction did funny things inside him. Or maybe it was that the plane was rolling. Unlike her, he loved the exhilaration of taking off and soaring through the air.

"If I hadn't been here, you'd have done the same thing. It's what you do every workday," she reminded him. "I didn't do anything out of the ordinary that any other health care professional couldn't have done."

"Other than be completely prepared for any emergency that came up while thirty thousand plus feet in the air?" he countered, knowing that he could argue that she'd done a lot of things out of the ordinary. Everything about Ivy McEwen was out of the ordinary.

She humphed. "I like to be prepared. Sometimes to the point that I drive those around me a bit crazy. Be forewarned." Her eyes challenged him, urging him to keep pushing. He told himself it was just because her tension lines had momentarily eased during their plane's taxiing to the runway.

"Were you a Girl Scout?" he teased.

"I was," she admitted, half smiling. "But just for a couple of years during early elementary school."

"Never sold cookies?"

She made a scoffing sound. "I sold cookies. Lots and lots of cookies."

Caleb liked that she was distracted from what the plane was doing. "That sounds as if there's a story there."

"I sold the most cookies of anyone in my troop."

He grinned. "Competitive much?"

"Maybe." Her eyes sparkled. "I like to always do my best. That's why I prep so much. I try to plan for success no matter what comes up. That I wasn't fully prepared for what happened with Bella is a bit frustrating."

"It's not as if you can travel with a full emergency room inventory. You impressed me. And it wasn't just me who was impressed. Everyone on this plane was grateful you were here, especially Bella and Tom." Despite how she white-knuckled her seat belt, Ivy's smile appeared genuine. Hoping she'd further relax and that maybe he truly could distract her through takeoff, he continued, "Comedy will have to be a side gig. Medicine is your calling."

She let out a relieved-sounding breath. "Phew, I was worried that I'd wasted all those years on med school."

Joy filled him at her teasing tone, and he laughed. "It's always good to have a plan B, but you're right where you're supposed to be."

Beside him.

The thought caught him off guard.

Not beside him.

Sure, he was attracted to her, but he was getting way ahead of himself. They'd just met. She was the kind of girl his mother would like him to bring home. These days, she'd settle for him to bring any girl home because, after his last split with Katrina, she claimed to have given up that he would ever settle down. He found that odd since he was only in his early thirties, but she'd been known to be dramatic in the past. In regard to his dating life, or lack thereof, was no exception. Then again, after Katrina, he'd certainly never given his mother a reason to think he'd ever "settle down."

"Thank you," Ivy said. "I like thinking I made the right choice when I chose to go into medicine."

Curiosity got him again. "What would you have chosen if not medicine?"

Before she could answer, the pilot came over the PA system, letting them know they were next in line, and they'd soon be on their way to Paris again. Ivy grimaced.

"Not a pilot or stewardess or paratrooper," she assured, grimacing. "I really don't like flying."

"Seriously? I never would have guessed," he teased, hoping that doing so would help. He'd thought he'd been semi-achieving distraction, but her face had lost all color.

Still, she frowned. "Be nice. Not everyone is crazy—I mean, *brave* enough to jump out of airplanes."

He'd never thought of jumping as being brave. Jumping was a passion, a pure happiness, a rush of adrenaline like no other. Nothing he'd ever done or experienced made him feel as alive as he did when he was free-falling through the atmosphere. Nothing was so quiet or so peaceful. Jumping put all of life into perspective. He missed that sensation so much he ached with it.

The plane moved into position to where they'd begin their ascent.

Ivy sucked in a deep breath, her throat visibly working as she swallowed hard.

"Are you dating anyone, Ivy?"

"What?" She sounded almost as surprised by his question as he was. He sure hadn't been thinking of asking the question. It just popped out of his mouth.

He went with the question because she certainly looked distracted. Plus, he found himself really wanting to know her answer. "Are you dating anyone?"

"Now is not the time to be asking me about my dating life."

"Because the plane isn't going to lift off if you aren't completely focused on it and intensely gripping your seat while squeezing your eyes closed?"

She narrowed her gaze. "Smarty-pants."

"Sometimes," he agreed. "You didn't answer. Is there someone special who is missing you while you're in France? Someone who makes your heart go pitter-patter and feel as if you're on top of the world?"

She snorted. "Not hardly and I'm planning to stay single." Turning to him, she frowned. "I know what you're doing, Caleb, and it's not working. I'm well aware that we're gaining speed and— Ooh!" She grabbed his arm, squeezing as they gained momentum.

"I must be doing a terrible job distracting you.

Let's see if I can do better." He leaned toward her and, eyes wide, she jerked back, but didn't let go of where she clenched his arm in a death grip.

"I don't think so, buster."

"What?" he asked, innocently, lips twitching. "What did you think I was about to do, Ivy?"

"You know exactly what I thought," she countered, her grip on his arm tightening as her eyes squinched together.

"I was just going to whisper an ancient Chinese proverb into your ear."

"Sure, you were." The wheels lifted from the runway, and she had another sharp intake of breath. "Tell me. Tell me now."

"That you're quite lovely when your face is pinched up like that?"

Her eyes shot open and her brows formed a V. "Are you making fun of me?"

"Only in the sense of teasing you, Ivy. People are afraid of different things. I'd never make fun of someone for something they were afraid of. Fear is an emotion real to all of us. It's just what triggers the fear that varies."

"What are you afraid of?"

Caleb thought back to the times in his life he'd been afraid. There had been many, such as the time when two of his buddies had collided midair, leaving one of the guys unconscious and in a free fall at seven thousand feet. As he'd guided his own body through the air toward him, he'd been scared that he was going to watch his friend die. Essentially, he had, but not that day. Blake's automatic activation device should have gone off if he hadn't regained consciousness and deployed his chute by the minimum feet. Caleb getting to him and deploying his reserve chute had bought him four thousand feet to regain consciousness. Thank God the chute opening had snapped Blake awake so he'd been able to safely get to the ground, then go out for a few days' hospital stay with a concussion. Blake should have gotten out after that, but had lived to die another day.

"Why do I get the feeling that the things running through your mind right now make my fear of flying seem paltry?" Relaxing her hold on his arm, Ivy interrupted the dark rabbit hole he'd been falling in to. A rabbit hole he sometimes struggled to claw his way back from. Yeah, much better not to go there as he couldn't change the past. He couldn't bring Blake back, nor take his place.

"We all have our demons to face."

"I agree with that in principle, but I'll go on record as still finding my fear of flying irrational considering statistics and things I do that aren't nearly as 'safe,' yet I never give them a second thought. I mean, I'm more likely to be struck by lightning than to be in a plane crash, yet I don't get panicky during storms." She looked directly into his eyes, and he knew her next words weren't going to be about herself. "Were you deployed during your time in the military?"

"Yes. Several times."

"I'm sorry."

Her soft words had him meeting her gaze. "What are you sorry for? No one forced me to enlist, Ivy. I volunteered for high-risk missions. That doesn't mean I never experienced fear." He'd just learned to keep fear secondary to logic and the will to survive.

"Whatever you were thinking… I shouldn't have sent your mind there. That's what I meant when I said I was sorry."

"I have no regrets regarding my time in the military." Other than that he wasn't still there, proudly serving his country. His ankle tweaked, reminding him of why he wasn't. Frustrated, he flexed his foot back and forth.

"That's good." Taking a deep breath, she glanced around the plane. Concern and a deep sense of responsibility showed in the way her big blue eyes noticeably touched on all the veterans within her visual field. "They're braver than I am. I feel so weak that I hate flying so much."

He suspected that her admission was a rare one and probably due to the fact that they were in the midst of her trigger. "There are a lot of folks on this plane who found you brave while you were saving Bella's life. Not everyone can remain calm during a crisis. People have different strengths and weaknesses. It's what keeps humanity going."

Her gaze met his and she gave him another one of those smiles that had firecrackers going off in his belly. "Thanks for not thinking me wimpy for something that even small children do without it bothering them. Sorry if I caused permanent damage to your arm."

He cleared his throat and repositioned within his seat. "No problem. I'll send you a bill if I have to see an orthopedist."

"You do that." Her lips twitched. "You should also tell me that ancient Chinese proverb."

He shook his head. "Nah, the moment has passed. I'm going to save that one for the flight home."

"Ugh, don't remind me." She glanced around the plane again, then pressed the screen on the seat in front of her. "I'm going to watch a movie. Why don't you see if you can get some sleep?"

Caleb would rather talk to her, but she was obviously done. "You'll wake me when you want to rest?"

Although she nodded, he doubted that she'd wake him. He got the impression Ivy had to be tough. What had happened to make her feel that way? That she always had to be strong and not reveal any vulnerability? Then again, who was he to judge? Not that he was really, just more of a curiosity about the beautiful woman sitting next to him. He closed his eyes. He'd rest while she watched her movie.

Caleb had always been able to fall asleep readily. He'd also always been able to remain somewhat aware of what was going on around him. It was something he'd appreciated during his service days. While on a plane next to a woman he found more attractive than he'd found anyone in a long time, if ever, being constantly aware of her was distracting from being able to let himself drift into sleep, though.

Especially when a couple of hours later, her head rested against his shoulder.

Something deep within him relaxed as he focused on the rhythmic in-and-out of her breath, on the sweet vanilla scent that he'd caught a whiff of earlier, but now would forever remind him of her. His peace felt so at odds with the tumult that gripped his stomach at her body against his.

Suspecting that if he stirred, she'd awaken, he kept still, wondering why having a stranger resting upon his shoulder felt so right, so simultaneously dangerous, and why keeping her there felt so imperative.

CHAPTER FOUR

"COME ON, ROY," Ivy told her veteran. "Let's walk around the restaurant." The convenience center was more like a high-end commercialized rest stop than a single restaurant. There were multiple dining options, a general store, a fancy coffee shop and a refueling station. Truly, a one-stop shop for travelers and locals alike. There were even picnic tables out back and a small playground for children to stretch their legs. "Slade, if your grandfather is finished eating, get him to walking, too. Between the flight and the bus ride, we all need to move as much as we can prior to the rest of our drive."

They'd landed in Paris, been met by a local veterans' group and were being bused the four hours to Normandy. Halfway there, they'd stopped for a restroom and food break. And to get everyone moving. She couldn't have them getting stiff from travel and then not being able to enjoy the rest of the trip. As horrific as why they'd originally been here many decades before was, this trip was about honoring their legacy in freeing France from the occupation and helping them find healing.

"Okay, Owen. You and Suzie have finished eating, too. Let's get to moving," Caleb encouraged, standing and sorting his trash to put into appropriate recycle bins. "Do I need to start another conga line?"

Laughing, Owen's great-granddaughter did a little upper body shimmy. "I mean, if you want to, I'd be happy to dance with you."

Uh-oh. The young woman was staring at Caleb with stars in her eyes. Or were those hearts? Caleb needed to be careful not to encourage her. She was barely twenty and still at university.

Hello. Who was Ivy to think Suzie didn't need to be encouraged? Ivy had been the one all up in Caleb's business when she'd awakened on the plane. Her face had been smashed against his shoulder. How could she have gone to sleep like that? Ha. It wasn't even the going to sleep that was the biggest issue. It was how she'd been snuggled against him that had her internally cringing. Even worse was the knowledge that he knew. He'd made sure the guys walked and went to the restroom at some point during her snooze. She hadn't slept well the night before in dread of the flight, but that was no excuse for zoning out. The veterans had all been fine, but still, she wasn't one to shirk her duties.

Caleb hadn't said a word, not to point out that she'd been slacking and he'd had to take over, nor about her using him for a pillow as Luke would certainly have done. Her ex always made sure she knew anytime she failed to live up to expectations. Maybe Caleb had just assumed that invading your seatmate's personal space was natural airplane behavior. For Ivy, there had been nothing natural about sleeping against him.

His shoulder had been strong. He hadn't seemed to mind, but Ivy hated that she'd done so. She prided herself on her self-reliance and didn't want to lean on anyone. What must he think about her? How embarrassing!

Soon, they were back on their bus and moving down the road. As each veteran had a family member that they sat by and Lara sat next to a board member, Ivy supposed it was natural that she had ended up next to Caleb on the twenty-person minibus. Short of supplanting someone's family member from next to one of the veterans, she was stuck with Caleb. Owen's granddaughter might volunteer for the swap.

"Did you notice Paul stumble on the curbside on our way out to the bus?" Caleb drew her gaze to him from where she'd been staring out at the French countryside. "He refused to use his cane. Slade stayed close but Paul didn't want any help. He almost fell."

"Yeah, I caught that and tried to stay a little

closer, just in case. Pride is in no short abundance." Her biggest worry was that something preventable might happen to one of the veterans.

Caleb nodded. "It's what's gotten them to this point in life. They all impress me. When Stan asked me to go, I'll admit, given their ages, I wasn't expecting such ambulatory, sharp-as-a-tack men. Most of the ninety-five-plus folks we transport at the ambulance service are bedridden and may or may not remember who they are. For that matter, most of the eighty-plus-year-olds are."

"You're right. These guys are amazing in their zest for living life and refusal to sit down and 'act their age.' My grandfather—" Her stomach took a dive as surely as if they were still on the plane and had hit turbulence. "He knew how much I hated flying and teased me about how he was going to hold my hand like he did when I was a little girl. Honestly, if it weren't for how he loved being a paratrooper, I'd think he felt the same about flying as I do. To my knowledge he never flew again after his discharge from the army. He always said there was nowhere else he'd rather be than on his farm with my grandmother."

His face held empathy. "Sounds as if it was a big deal for both of you that you were planning this trip together."

"We were looking forward to it and dreading it at the same time." Ready for the personal conversation to end, she twisted to peer through the space between the window and seat. "How are you doing, Paul? You and Slade good?"

The former Higgins boat driver nodded, as did his great-grandson. Paul had been back to Normandy once, a couple of years previously, but this was his first time with his grandson. After a minute of light conversation about the beautiful French hillside and the minibus's robust air-conditioning, Ivy straightened in her seat and closed her eyes.

After they traveled the remaining two hours to their first stop in Sainte-Mère-église, the bus parked. French host families where the veterans would be staying during the trip greeted them. Introductions were made, and, travel weary, the guys and their family members took off with each of their hosts.

"I feel weird now that they're gone." Ivy glanced around the now vacant area, then smiled at her and Caleb's host family. Another had taken Lara and the board member. "We can drive to them if they have any issues, but part of me wants to keep them all within sight."

"And well cushioned with some bubble wrap?" Caleb teased.

"They are in good families' homes," Phillipe, their fiftyish host said in excellent English. Most of the local veterans group who'd met them had spoken at least some English. Most had been fairly fluent, like Phillipe. Phillipe had thick salt-and-pepper hair, warm brown eyes and a quick smile. "Come. I will show you where I live."

Phillipe insisted upon helping with Ivy's bags as they walked the two blocks to his home where he and his wife ran a bed-and-breakfast. Once at the close-to-the-road home, with its stone walls, steeply pitched slate roof and gorgeous red geraniums beneath the street side windows, his bundle of energy wife, Delphine, greeted them with cheek kisses. "Bonjour. Welcome."

Delphine's short wavy hair was streaked with gray, and her lovely face was lined from years of too much sun. Dimples dug into her cheeks each time she smiled, which was often. Ivy instantly adored her.

The home's inside was a mixture of stone and timber. The furniture looked sturdy and comfortable. The scent of something delightful, perhaps fresh baked bread, filled the house and had Ivy's stomach grumbling although it hadn't been but a few hours since their food stop. Apparently, there were two sections to the home's upper levels. The bed-and-breakfast's other guests were in one section and Caleb and Ivy in a smaller section.

They were shown their respective rooms. Caleb's was closest to the stairs, and Ivy waited in the hallway as Delphine led him into the bedroom with an antique bed. Their hostess pointed out where the shared bathroom was in the hallway, then showed Ivy a charming room with a heavy brass bed covered with a handmade quilt. Similar to Caleb's room, there was a lovely wardrobe and chair with an extra quilt draped over its armrest. The rooms could have looked the same a hundred years prior save the lighting and electrical outlets.

"Everything is beautiful, like stepping back in time," she told Delphine. Her hostess looked pleased that she liked the rooms, then headed back downstairs, leaving Ivy to unpack.

The remainder of the day had been set aside for getting acquainted with one's host family so all the veterans were fully occupied, leaving Ivy out of sorts as she felt she should be checking on them. She unpacked and settled into her room, used the shared bathroom and then went downstairs to where Delphine was in the process of preparing a meal. Delphine refused help, insisting that Ivy was her guest, and it was her honor to feed her.

In the living area, Phillipe was showing Caleb his collection of World War II memorabilia. The Frenchman very proudly told of veterans his family had hosted during previous D-Day anniversaries, proclaiming great honor in the privilege. Ivy couldn't help but wonder if the couple felt cheated by hosting her and Caleb rather than a veteran.

Regardless, the couple were wonderfully friendly, charming in their accents and happy looks at one another. There were three other guest couples. Two American and one British. All were there for the D-Day events. Their dinner was excellent and the company entertaining. Phillipe had pulled out a 1944 wine to commemorate their arrival. Ivy didn't usually drink, but her hosts had been so proud of the special bottle, she'd taken a small glass of the woodsy red liquid and was slowly sipping the delicious vintage.

"You're a couple?" one of the American women asked. Trista and her husband were in their late fifties, as were the other two couples. They all seemed to be well acquainted.

Even though she knew it was a natural assumption, Ivy's cheeks heated. "No. We just met this morning at the Knoxville airport. We're medical volunteers for a veteran group."

"Ah, that's wonderful on the volunteering. We've been here for a week. We volunteer annually at one of the reenactments. Fred looks forward to our time here more than anything else we do during our retirement."

"That's great. How many years have you been coming?" Ivy was grateful that the conversation hadn't lingered on Caleb. Odd to think they really had met less than twenty-four hours prior. Then again, it had been a long, eventful day of constant togetherness.

"This is our twenty-fifth year coming for the D-Day anniversary. We visited for a vacation one year early on in our marriage. The first time we came, we became good friends with some people who were involved with the reenactments. Most stay in tents on-site. We usually do a few key nights, as well. But I prefer Phillipe and Delphine's. This gal is over sleeping on an uncomfortable cot," the woman laughed, obviously being hit with memories.

"We love having you and Fred visit each year." Delphine topped off Trista's wineglass.

The two women chatted about past stays, the other female guests chiming in as they were apparently also repeat guests. Fighting fatigue and perhaps the wine catching up with her, Ivy listened, smiling frequently. The men were in a hardy discussion regarding whether or not the paratrooper jump at the end of the week would end up being rescheduled as rain was predicted for the scheduled date. The two American men were both retired military, as was the British gentleman. Although he was young enough to be their son, Caleb still fit right in with his military background. Head tossed back, he laughed at something one of them said.

"He's quite handsome, your fellow."

"Truly, we just met this morning," she reminded, cheeks on fire. "He seems a great guy, but I barely know him."

The women exchanged a look and just smiled. "Paris may be the City of Love, but it is because the country of France opens one's heart to the possibility of *amour*. You'll see, Normandy is no different."

Mortified at the conversation in case the men were paying even the slightest attention to what the women were saying, Ivy shook her head. "Nope. Not interested in *amour*. I just finished my residency and moved back to Tennessee to start working at a hospital's emergency department." Plus, she had to figure out what she was going to do with her grandfather's farm. She didn't have the heart to sell it, but she didn't want it to deteriorate. So much love and sweat and tears had gone in to working the land over the years. It was a part of who she was. But what was she going to do with hundreds of acres of farmland? She didn't want to think about that right now. Or ever, really. She wanted Gramps there, working the land and adding his own sunshine to the world. Tears prickled her eyes, and she fought swiping at them. She couldn't and not have Delphine and Trista convinced that their love conversation had brought her to tears. If it had, it would be for the time she'd wasted in the name of "love."

"Which hospital will you be working for?"

A fresh heat wave spread across Ivy's face. Caleb had heard the women's comments. Had he been internally laughing at her emphatic denial of interest in him? Yep, she was mortified. Then again, he'd been the one to ask if she was dating anyone. Of course, that had probably just been an attempt to distract her during takeoff rather than any true interest in her relationship status.

"Knoxville General."

He grinned. "Our paths are destined to cross again after we return home."

Curious, but trying not to look too much so under the ladies' watchful eyes, Ivy arched a brow. "Do you make emergency calls? I thought you worked for a private ambulance service."

"I do, and one of the places we transport patients is to your hospital. Nonemergency trips, but we seem to be in and out of the ER frequently." He grinned. "I look forward to continuing our new friendship after we return to the States."

She couldn't see them being BFFs, but she enjoyed talking to him and had she not embarrassed herself by falling asleep on his shoulder, she'd say it had been a great experience.

"One can never have too many friends," she said for the benefit of their curious audience. "It'll be good to see a familiar face from time to time." Other than those she'd met during the hiring process she knew very few people in Knoxville. She'd met a few of her grandfather's friends, but most of them were her parents' age or older. And, then there were those she'd met through SMVF that she likely would remain friends with. Why would Caleb be any different from the rest of the group with whom she'd already bonded?

The meal lasted over two hours and was still going strong when fatigue won over Ivy. Her eyelids had grown too heavy to keep fighting them.

"Sorry to call it a night so early—" which it was by the clock "—but the traveling is taking its toll and I'm ready to get some sleep. I will see you all in the morning, sooner if any of our guys or their families need anything. Night."

The men, including Caleb, all stood, showing their manners. The women bid her goodnight. Ivy used the restroom she shared with Caleb, cleansing her face, brushing her teeth, then returning to snuggle beneath the covers of the antique bed. Her room was small by American standards, but well decorated with beautiful antiques that had been in Delphine's family for many decades.

Thinking of the furniture at the farm that had been her great-grandparents', Ivy sighed. Someday, if she did meet someone who could lift her up to their level rather than try to tear her down, got married and had children, she'd want them to walk the land her great-grandparents had. She'd want them to play in the creek her grandmother, mother and herself had once caught crawdads in and swam in the deep spots to cool from the hot Tennessee sun. She'd want them to sleep in the bed that had belonged to their family for over a hundred years.

But, oh, the thought of how lonely she'd be on

the farm without her beloved Gramps beside her, to hear him moving about the kitchen, making his coffee at the crack of dawn before heading out to check on the cattle that no longer belonged to him, but rather a neighbor who leased the land. Ivy would need to talk to Mr. Griggs to see if he wanted to continue doing so after his current lease expired. She'd want all the help she could get in paying the taxes on the place. Then again, there was the trust her grandfather had left, as well. Her mother wasn't too happy that Gramps had, for the most part, bypassed his only living child, and left his worldly goods to his sole great-grandchild. Ivy wasn't sure of his reasons and certainly had never encouraged him to do such. In some ways, his leaving the farm to her mother would have been easier, although heartbreaking as her mother would have had no hesitations in selling the place.

Ivy couldn't do that. Perhaps Gramps had known and that's why he'd made the decisions he had. Ivy would live there and keep the land he'd loved for as long as she had breath and ability to do so. The farm was in her blood, a part of her past and a part of who she was.

She couldn't help wondering what Caleb would think of the white farmhouse that's walls had seen such love, and the land that had provided for her family for multiple generations. Why was it that she could imagine him there, at the house and walking the fields with the Smoky Mountains off in the distance? Would he hold the rich soil in his palm and feel the soul of the land? Would he understand or think her crazy for keeping something that would be a lot of work to maintain even with leasing the farmland?

What was wrong with her? Her thoughts were insane ramblings of a woman too weary from travel and too much wine. Just the one glass, but when she usually didn't drink, those were the things she was blaming for her thoughts. Blaming for her dreams.

That, and that alone, was the reason she drifted to sleep with the image of walking hand in hand with Caleb Rivers, a man she'd just met, across the fields at her great-grandfather's farm, and a sense of peace at his being by her side.

CHAPTER FIVE

"GOOD MORNING," CALEB greeted Ivy as she came down the narrow steps leading into the living area of Phillipe and Delphine's bed-and-breakfast. She wore black pants with side pockets and a navy T-shirt with the SMVF logo across the chest. Her hair was in a fresh braid and her cheeks were rosy as if she'd just washed her face. "Coffee?"

She smiled as if he'd offered her a great treasure. "That would be amazing."

He got a bowl from where Delphine had shown him. Ivy glanced at it in question.

"Bowls, not mugs. It's so you can dip your bread in your coffee." When she still stared at him, he grinned. "Just go with it. Cream? Sugar?" he asked as he filled the bowl, hiding his surprise when she shook her head. He would have guessed her to be a cream and sugar partaker. "Phillipe headed out this morning to deliver some of Delphine's goodies to a few other bed-and-breakfasts. He should be back any moment. Delphine is outdoors cutting fresh flowers for her bouquet. She has a garden out back. She said to tell you to help yourself to breakfast if you came down prior to her coming back indoors."

"Her flowers are gorgeous. I noticed them out my window." Taking the steaming mug he handed her, Ivy took a tentative sip, then sighed her pleasure. "I don't eat much bread, much less dip it in my coffee, but Delphine's smells heavenly."

"The bread is wonderful, but I'm with you on dipping it in my coffee. I recommend using the butter and jam. Delphine cans the jam and the butter comes from the same neighbor where she buys her milk."

Ivy placed her coffee bowl on the table, then went to Delphine's morning spread. "Wow."

She looked like a kid on Christmas morning. He grinned. "Just wait until you taste."

When she'd applied butter and jam to her bread, she licked her jam spoon and her eyes widened. "Yum. That *is* good."

Watching her put the spoon in her mouth, Caleb fought to rein in his gut reaction to the innocent action. "I told you."

"Good thing we're only here for two weeks or I'd have to buy a new wardrobe." She took a bite of the doctored bread, then her face relaxed with pure joy. "Mmm… I may have to anyway. This is worth it."

Ivy's sigh of pleasure did funny things to Caleb's insides, like twist him into knots. He gulped back the one that formed in his throat and reached for the bread. "You make that look so good I'm going to have a second slice."

"You better hurry. If you don't, there won't be any left," she teased. "For real, I may hide what's left in my room."

Caleb chuckled. "Apparently, she does this every morning for their guests and sells loaves to other hosts in the area as an income supplement. Delphine says the communities in the area are very interdependent upon each other, buying from local farmers and vendors and supporting each other."

"I love that. With everything being so fresh, no wonder it tastes so wonderful." She took another bite and moaned. "This reminds me of when I was small and would visit my grandparents. The flavors are so rich."

Almost choking on his bread, Caleb cleared his throat. "Um, yeah, Phillipe should be back so we can head to the school for our first program."

Still enjoying her bread, she glanced at her watch. "Did I run late? It's just after seven and I thought we had plenty of time."

Caleb slid his fingers into his jeans pocket. "We do."

Her brow lifted. "Is the school far away, then?"

"Not far. We should arrive in plenty of time since we're not due until ten. The board purposely didn't schedule anything early this morning so that the veterans could have a later start in case any of them experience jet lag. Or if we did. Or, well, you know." What was wrong with him? He wasn't one to ramble, but that's certainly what he was doing. He felt like an awkward teenage boy talking to the homecoming queen. "The other guests won't be here for dinner tonight and Phillipe thought we might enjoy dinner with him and Delphine at a friend's who lives along the coast."

Ivy took another bite of her bread. "I don't want them to go to any trouble."

"I got the impression he hoped we'd say yes. Paul and Slade are staying there, and they've invited Owen and Suzie, as well."

Ivy's gaze met his, but she didn't say anything.

"What?" he asked, knowing something was on her mind.

"I was just trying to decide if that's why you wanted to go."

Confused, he asked, "If what was why I wanted to go?"

"Suzie."

Shock filled him. She thought— Seriously? "You're kidding, right?"

She studied him a moment, then a slow smile

spread across her face. "Oh, I don't know. She's beautiful."

"And young."

"As long as both parties are of legal age and of normal mental capabilities, then age is just a number."

"I agree up to a certain point." He noted how her gaze never shifted from his as she took a sip of her coffee. "Would you date someone a lot younger or older than you, Ivy?"

She considered his question, then shrugged. "As long as my conditions were met, I would if I was attracted to him. Maybe I even should since dating men around my own age hasn't worked out too well."

Curious, Caleb started to ask her to elaborate on what her conditions were and what had gone wrong with the men she'd dated, but Delphine came in, her hands full of colorful flowers.

"Oh, the zinnias are beautiful," Ivy praised, eyeing the blooms. "And, Delphine, this bread is the best I've ever put in my mouth. The texture and flavor are perfection. It literally melts in my mouth."

Placing her flowers on the counter, Delphine beamed. "*Merci.* I've been making bread since I was a little girl. It was my *grandmère*'s recipe."

Caleb watched the two women chat, helping himself to more bread as he did so. When Ivy had finished eating, she offered to assist Delphine, but the Frenchwoman shooed her away, just as she'd done to Caleb earlier. He'd be sure to leave a generous tip and in-depth review online as a way of saying thank you.

Phillipe returned, asking if they could be ready to leave within the hour. Ivy disappeared upstairs for about fifteen minutes, came back down with her backpack. Caleb had grabbed his, as well. He doubted he had anything Ivy didn't other than his defibrillator, but as they'd learned on the plane, one never knew. They headed for the middle school where the veterans would be speaking that morning. They left early, so Phillipe drove them by Brécourt Manor, stopping to look at the 101st Airborne memorial at the edge of the private property. Other than the memorial to the brave paratroopers who'd taken out the four-gun battery aimed at Utah Beach, the area appeared like ordinary farmland. It would be easy to drive past without realizing unless one knew its history. Caleb knew. The brave men of Easy Company were legendary and had fueled his desire to be a paratrooper. The 101st no longer jumped, so joining the Eighty-Second had been a no-brainer. They were all his brothers-in-arms.

Caleb dug through his medical backpack, found a package of wipes and cleaned the yellowy-green pollen film from the top of the monument.

"Much better." He turned back toward where

Ivy stood with Phillipe. Appreciation for what he'd done shone in her gaze. A gaze that burned so blue it shamed the sky above them.

"Yes. It is," she agreed. "Thank you for doing that."

Caleb shrugged but was pleased at her sincerity. She understood where they were, what they were seeing. Perhaps she just recognized the area from the television series from several years prior, but she seemed to hold true empathy for the men whose names were on the stone. With having been so close to her great-grandfather who'd been a WWII paratrooper, perhaps she did.

Phillipe returned to the car, but only to lean against it.

Running his gaze over the land, images filled Caleb's head. Images that transformed from the men who were there into Caleb's team from—Yeah, it was time to leave. Spinning, he moved toward the car.

Back in the car, Ivy eyed him, then to his surprise, she touched his hand. When his gaze met hers, she gave him another one of those empathetic looks.

"This place can really get to you, can't it?" she whispered.

"There were voices on the wind, as if those men who died were calling to us from the past."

Her eyes shone with surprise. "I felt it, too."

They arrived at the school, joined the others

who were just arriving, and were welcomed by the French children and the school's staff. Then the veterans were set up at the front of the cafeteria.

When they were done, Caleb spoke with one of the teachers and every so often glanced around, taking in where each of the veterans were and how the children surrounded them, asking questions, some having to be interpreted, and the ones who owned phones wanting to take selfies with them. Ivy stood close with a bottle of hand sanitizer which she shared with the children and frequently with veterans, obviously determined to do all she could to keep the guys from picking up germs. Smiling, she chatted with the children, asking questions and praising their efforts to speak in English.

After the kids had gotten a chance to meet the veterans and get photos with them, a few gave a tour of the school and how they'd prepared for the veterans' visit. Ivy and Caleb fell to the back of the group.

"What amazing children and teachers," Ivy whispered, echoing his thoughts. "This place makes me want to go to school here."

"None of my schools had a garden or chickens." This one had both.

A commotion at the front of the crowd instantly had him and Ivy rushing to see what was happening.

A long verbal string of French, doubtful that it was cursing given none of the children reacted, came from an older woman sitting on the floor. She shooed the students back with one hand as her other grasped at her leg. Blood stained her fingers.

"Here's Dr. Ivy and Caleb now." Mary waved them closer. "This retired teacher volunteered today. She tripped and fell against Dad's wheelchair. I'm not sure what she cut herself on, though, as there's not anything sharp."

The teacher said more in French and another interpreted. "She says it's just a scrape. No big deal. She doesn't want a fuss." The interpreter eyed the injured teacher's leg. "That's a lot of blood, though."

Ivy already knelt next to the retired teacher and was unzipping her backpack.

"Tell her that we won't make a big deal of it, but I want to check her leg and clean the area for her." Ivy donned a pair of gloves and grabbed some supplies. "Here, let me see what's causing the bleeding."

The woman removed her hand from her leg. Whatever she'd hit had avulsed the skin, possibly from tension, and peeled it to a crinkled bunch at the wound's edge. Caleb knelt and put on a pair of gloves, too. Ivy had already started cleaning the wound. One thing he'd learned about Ivy was that she preferred being in charge and dived right in when there was a medical issue. Was she that way in other aspects of life? He didn't think so. If anything, he suspected she overthought everything.

Ivy carefully smoothed the pushed back skin into place. "Tell her that fortunately the injury isn't too deep. I'm going to use adhesive strips and then will cover the area with a protective dressing."

Serving as her "clean" hands, Caleb got the items from her backpack.

"She'll have a scar," Ivy continued. "But I suspect it will barely be visible a year or so from now."

One of the other teachers translated for the injured woman, who then shook her head and said something back. "She says she is a clumsy oaf and is embarrassed at the attention."

"Assure her that there's no reason to be embarrassed. Anyone can trip." Smiling her appreciation, Ivy took his offerings. "Will you ask if she is allergic to anything? Adhesives or latex bandages, specifically?"

The interpreter asked, then advised there were no allergies.

"Good. We've had enough allergic reactions this trip." Caleb opened the packet of the adhesive strips and gave them to her.

"Thanks." She glanced up just long enough to meet his gaze, sending his pulse into hyperdrive.

"Help me keep the skin pushed together while I apply the strips?"

"Sure thing, Doc." Caleb kept the wound edges together while she removed a strip then pressed it on the torn skin. She meticulously repeated the process until she had the wound closed. After she'd pressed the last one into place, he covered the area with a dressing. He secured his work with a self-adherent wrap.

"Good as new," he proclaimed when he finished.

"*Merci*," the woman thanked them. "*Merci beaucoup.*"

"Yes, *merci beaucoup*," Ivy repeated, causing Caleb's gaze to go back to hers. She smiled and, in that moment, something stirred deep inside him that made him want to kiss her.

Although, if he were honest with himself, he'd admit that he'd been wanting to kiss Ivy from the moment he'd met her gaze at the airport and recognized something in those blue eyes that he still didn't quite understand.

After they'd finished the morning's events at the elementary school, Ivy and Caleb traveled back to Sainte-Mère-église with Phillipe. They met with the others from their group at the courtyard in front of the Notre-Dame-de-l'Assomption. As Phillipe and Delphine lived in the village, they'd passed the famous church with its "paratrooper" hanging from the bell tower several times. The chute's white material flapped in the wind, a reminder of the events that had once taken place there.

Goose bumps covered Ivy's skin and not for the first time that day. After they'd repaired the teacher's laceration, Caleb had made her goose bumps have goose bumps. The intensity of his gaze triggered the response. He'd looked at her as if she were dipped in chocolate and he was a starving dessert-aholic.

He was pointing to the parachute, no doubt asking Owen about his experiences on D-Day. His sunglasses glinted in the sunshine. His T-shirt wasn't tight, but the sleeves stretched slightly over his biceps. No doubt finding T-shirts that fit his chest but didn't swallow his narrow waist wasn't easy. Perhaps sensing her stare, he looked her way and smiled. She couldn't see his eyes, but his smile was the one that she knew put a twinkle in them. Had he known she was checking him out and essentially drooling?

"Ready to go inside the church?" She linked her arm with Paul's. She needed to get out of the sun as it was frying her brain. Or maybe it was Caleb frying her brain. Chatting as they went, they slowly made their way to Notre-Dame-de-l'Assomption. Once inside, the beauty of the ornate, but musty-smelling, building struck her. Weathered white stone walls and aged arches surrounded well-worn benches, yet the front of the church was elaborate: a gold arch hanging from the ceiling with a cross mounted to the top and an intricate painting, ornate golden trimming, and a beautiful altar. The contrast seemed at odds and yet somehow perfectly fit the church.

"This place was built to stand forever." Slade joined Ivy and his grandfather. "They don't build them like this anymore, do they, Grandpa?"

"Not that I'm aware of." Paul took in their surroundings.

The church did look as if it had been standing forever and as if it would still be there long after they'd passed.

"These days it seems many are built to be more beautiful on the outside, rather than focused on what's inside. I appreciate this way more," she mused to the veteran, Slade, Mary and Roy who had joined them. "Plain on the outside and stunning once you go through the doors."

"Ivy, will you take mine and Dad's picture with the altar in the background?" Mary handed her phone to Ivy, then posed next to Roy.

Ivy snapped a few shots, then a few of Slade and Paul. Then, they perused and were awed by the church for a few more minutes prior to the board member rounding them up. "Come on, guys. It's time for our tour of the Airborne Museum."

The museum was walking distance across the

courtyard, but they insisted the veterans ride in wheelchairs. None of them were too pleased, but they did so with only Owen grumbling in protest. Once they arrived at the museum, he was immediately up and out of the chair. Ivy smiled at his determination and was proud he was that way. The more he moved in life, the longer he'd be able to.

They toured the museum. She couldn't look at any of the displays without thinking that they reflected a portion of her grandfather's life. He'd been in the Eighty-Second, rather than the 101st, but both units endured great hardships. Ivy snapped several photos of the guys, crew and the many displays, some of which squeezed her heart tightly with awe and renewed appreciation for her great-grandfather and for her freedom. Pausing at a display of a wedding gown, she read the placard.

"Isn't that just the most romantic thing?" Mary came to stand beside Ivy. "That he saved and carried his parachute around until he could ship it home so he could ask his girlfriend to marry him and she could use the silk to have her wedding dress made? Just the thought of some man doing that for me makes me all giddy inside. Can you imagine?"

No, Ivy couldn't. Not really. She'd seen photos of her great-grandparents on their wedding day and best she could recall, the plain silk dress hadn't once been a life-saving parachute. But it wouldn't have surprised her had her great-grand-father done something similar. He'd loved Grammie so much and been so proud of his service that any meshing of the two would have made sense.

"Simple and yet so absolutely perfect," she agreed.

"I doubt many women would go for a dress made from a parachute these days."

"I would." It was true. "I can't imagine any-thing more special than to give myself to a man I loved while wearing something that had been vital in bringing him home to me."

Mary gave a look of approval. "Me, too, not that I'm in the market for another wedding. I can't imagine my husband having carried around a parachute just so I could wear it, but he's a good guy. We've been together for almost forty years."

"Forty years is a major accomplishment," Ivy praised.

"It's not always been easy, but I can't imag-ine life without him." Mary shifted her gaze to the men joining them. "What about you, Caleb? You were a paratrooper. Did you save one of your chutes so that you can have your bride make a wedding dress from it?"

Ivy's cheeks burned at Mary's question, which was quite silly as it was an innocent enough ques-tion and Caleb didn't seem to mind her having asked.

Chuckling, he shook his head. "I didn't save any of my chutes. Unlike during the Second World War when parachutes were made from silk, the chutes I jumped with were made from nylon, which is what most chutes these days are made from. I doubt any woman would want a nylon wedding dress."

"Oh, I don't know," Mary countered. "As with back then, knowing the material had saved your beloved's life definitely makes a difference to the right woman."

"Saving his chute may have had more to do with rations and the price of silk than romance." Ivy was ready to move on from the conversation. Talking about weddings with Caleb made her palms clammy. Mary had said he was single. Had there been a time when there was someone special in his life? Someone that, had his chute been silk, he'd have saved the precious material in hopes she'd wear it to walk down the aisle to him? Or maybe he had been married and no longer was? *Single* could mean a lot of things.

What do I want it to mean?

Nothing. Her fingers curled into her palms. She was not interested in Caleb's love life, past or present.

"You're probably right," Caleb agreed. "Saving his parachute was likely the only way his bride would have a silk gown unless they were wealthy. Carrying that chute around saved him a lot of money. Smart guy."

"Maybe," Mary conceded. "But I like my way better. Yours isn't nearly as romantic as a besotted beau carrying around his chute so his beloved can become his wife while wearing a dress made from it."

"You a hopeless romantic, Mary?" Caleb teased.

The woman nodded. "Absolutely. It's one of my greatest personality traits. I get it from Dad."

Caleb laughed. "Does Roy know you just called him a hopeless romantic?"

So ready to move on from wedding conversation, Ivy pointed to another display. "Speaking of Roy, I'm going to check on him and the other guys."

Because she wasn't a hopeless romantic or anything close. Yet, she had just told Mary she would have worn a dress made from her beloved's parachute, so that meant her having struck out three times hadn't left her impervious to romance. She would have preferred imperviousness.

That evening, restlessness hit while waiting to leave for Phillipe and Delphine's friend's home.

Perhaps feeling the same, Caleb asked, "I think I'm going to walk around town, maybe check out a local pub and have a drink. Do you want to join me, Doc?"

Ivy didn't want to waste a precious moment of

being in France. She might never be again, and wanted to see and do all she could. That was why she said, "I'd love to."

CHAPTER SIX

WITH IVY AT his side, Caleb wandered along the streets, checking out the touristy shops, going in to several to look for souvenirs.

When he selected several cool key chains, Ivy arched a brow. "You must have a lot of friends."

"They're for my coworkers at TransCare. I plan to pick up a few at different places and bring them back for the crew."

"That's nice of you to bring something back for them."

"You're sounding a little condescending there, Ivy," he teased as they headed to the front of the store.

Still wearing her practical black pants with zipper pockets on the side and bright blue SMVF T-shirt that made the color of her eyes pop, Ivy shrugged. "I'm not a huge fan of tourist trinkets."

"No way." He gave her a dubious look. "Key chains, spoons and snow globes don't excite you?"

She curled her nose.

He laid the assorted key rings on the counter. "Elaborate because I know there's more to that look than just simply not liking travel mementos."

Her brow arched. "You're not buying that I think they're an overpriced waste of money?"

"Perhaps," he agreed. "But then, how do you put a price tag on letting someone know they were special enough for you to have thought of them?"

She gave him an "Are you for real?" look.

"You don't bring back travel goodies? Not even for close friends and family?"

She shook her head. "My parents traveled a lot. Without me." She sighed. "You know my embarrassing reason for not going with them. They'd bring back magnets, postcards, T-shirts, snow globes, that kind of thing. I have quite the collection."

Imagining her with a box full of trinkets, he grinned. "Well, you obviously liked the mementos a little if you saved them."

"Oh, no. It's not really that I saved them, but that my parents did. They're boxed up in my old room's closet at their house, so definitely not prized possessions that I've hauled with me to school or residency moves." She tapped the edge of the cashier counter, then picked up one of his key chains, studying it. "My parents meant well. I just never saw the point of bringing back a gift labeled with a place where the recipient hadn't been, you know?"

That sort of made sense to Caleb, but not so much that he put the key chains back. Instead, he pulled out his credit card. "They probably wanted you to see all the places you were missing out on and hoped you'd push through your fear of flying."

"They didn't stand a chance of that because I got to stay with Gramps when they traveled. In my eyes, it was a win-win. No flying *and* visiting my favorite person in the world for the summer. I'd have found a reason to stay with him if they'd tried to force me to go. I loved being with him on the farm."

He handed the cashier his card, then glanced at Ivy. Her gaze had gone beyond him to stare out the window, her thoughts obviously far away. "You speak of him with such adoration. He must have been a great person."

"He was." She took a deep breath, glanced around the shop, then motioned to the door. "I'll be out there when you finish with your tourist bling."

When Caleb had paid for the key chains, he found Ivy on the sidewalk taking a selfie with a soldier statue in front of another shop. The silliness surprised him. He hadn't taken her for a selfie-taking girl, especially not after how serious her expression had been.

They stopped at a pub. He ordered a beer and Ivy a lemonade. The place was crowded with young soldiers also there for the anniversary events. Watching them, their camaraderie, hit Caleb with such nostalgia that he downed his drink. He hadn't expected to be struck with such longing.

From where she sat next to him at a table across from the bar, Ivy poked his arm. "Thirsty?"

"Not anymore."

She eyed him curiously, letting him know that she was aware that his "thirst" hadn't been normal. She didn't pry, just sat next to him, sipping her lemonade and people watching the noisy crowd.

Caleb took in the wall decor featuring soldiers and past anniversary celebrations. But his focus was torn between where they were and how he felt such a part of the events and yet felt so distanced from them as well, then jumping to where Ivy sat quietly taking it all in, and his being so aware of her that it was as if her light vanilla scent beckoned every cell within him even through the crowded pub.

What a wonderful and complex woman she was with her box of tourist trinkets, idolized grandfather, brilliant mind, skilled hands and generous heart.

"I asked before but didn't get a direct answer.

Is there someone you aren't buying a tourist trinket for, Ivy, but that you should be?"

Her gaze cut to him. "No, Caleb, there's no one in my life in need of a key chain. I've alluded to my poor dating habits of the past and have no desire to add another round." She finished off her lemonade with almost the same gusto he'd shown earlier, then stood. "Come on, Caleb. Let's head to Phillipe and Delphine's so we can get ready to go to dinner at their friends' home."

The next few days passed quickly. Their mornings were filled with scheduled activities for the veterans, each one visiting a school to speak to students and answer their questions, often via an interpreter. Each day, Ivy was more and more impressed and intrigued by the man who made her smile more than she'd dreamed possible. She didn't want to like Caleb so much, but she couldn't help it. He was intelligent, quick-witted and oozed pheromones that had her insides all aflutter.

In Colleville-sur-Mer, they met up with a larger World War II veteran organization who'd brought forty precious veterans and one female nurse veteran for the celebrations. A former NBA player had started the foundation. He and his wife traveled with the group, overseeing every aspect to make sure everyone was taken excellent care of by the many volunteers with their organization.

Ivy was impressed and enjoyed meeting the veterans, the volunteers and the locals who worked so diligently to make sure all the events went smoothly. She was also impressed with how Caleb interacted with each one, shaking their hand and sharing obvious mutual respect from one soldier to another. With the way she'd idolized Gramps, she should have known she'd be attracted to someone with a military background. It made sense, especially when they were in this unique, almost surreal world of Normandy where their veterans were treated with the same recognition as movie stars were back home. They were treated as the heroes they truly were. No wonder her insides were all mushy.

They visited the museum, then the American Cemetery. A small ceremony took place at the memorial where children presented gifts to the veterans. Lots of photos and media interviews were done. Then, they strolled through the cemetery grounds.

The American Cemetery was a humbling place that overlooked Omaha Beach where so many had died on June 6, 1944. The enormity that each of the precisely placed crosses represented a person who had lost their life in the name of freedom wasn't lost on Ivy. She wavered between her own emotional reaction to the nine thousand plus crosses and remaining aware of where each of her veterans were being rolled by their host families on the walkway through the grounds. They'd given up protesting using the wheelchairs as many of the places they visited covered too far of a distance for them to ambulate the entire time. As always, Owen stood each time they came to a stop. The man was as independent as he was a flirt. She imagined he'd been something else during his heyday.

Speaking of men in their heyday, where was Caleb? Glancing around, Ivy spotted him knelt at one of the crosses. The set of his jaw was tense. She was too far away to read his eyes even if his sunglasses hadn't shaded them, but she suspected she knew what they held. She understood. Curious as to whose cross Caleb stared at, she motioned to Lara.

"Keep an eye on the guys. I'll be right back." Not waiting for a response, she took off to where Caleb was and respectfully approached him. The wind caught at his SMVF shirt, plastering the cotton material to his bowed shoulders and chest. Her fingers itched to touch him. In comfort, she assured herself. That was why she wanted to put her hands upon his arm. No other reason.

"Someone you knew?" She took in the name and state engraved upon the marker.

Seeming surprised she was there, Caleb shook his head. "Never heard of him." He took a deep breath. "But I could have had I been around during that time, you know?"

Ivy's stomach squeezed. "Had you been around during that time one of these crosses could have had your name on it."

She quivered, then wondered about the nine thousand plus who were buried there. Most had been so young they'd barely begun their lives. They had left behind mothers and fathers who had mourned them. Left behind girlfriends they might have become engaged to and someday married and had families of their own. The knot in Ivy's stomach tightened further. There was so much she took for granted each day. Her freedom being one of the many.

"Thank you for your service, Caleb." For a moment, she thought her words were lost in the wind coming off the ocean just beyond the cliff overlooking the beach.

Caleb's head bowed. "Don't thank me. Not here. My service was nothing compared to what these guys did."

"You'd have done the same, would have willingly given your life that day had you been here." It was true. She'd only met him a few days ago, but that Caleb was as patriotic as they came oozed from his every pore. The thought of his having done that, of his life having been snuffed out, gripped her insides and twisted, making her nauseous. Her knees wobbled so much that she wouldn't have been surprised if she landed next to his feet.

"Many of these guys weren't necessarily willingly here," he reminded her. "Many of them were drafted and had no choice."

"The paratroopers were all volunteers, though." Gramps had told her that. Thank God he'd survived the war.

"For an extra hundred dollars' pay a month." Sighing, Caleb glanced around the somber graveyard with its white crosses, memorial and chapel. The wind whipped at an American flag that stood near the memorial reflecting pool and held his attention. "After Pearl Harbor, there was a flurry of enlistees, but over the next few years, many more were drafted. War is hell. Then, and now."

The wind lifted his words and carried them through the trees lining the pathway, swaying branches and rustling leaves. Ivy shivered, but not from the crispness of the breeze. "It's difficult for you to be here, isn't it?"

A *humph* sound rose from deep in his throat as he stood. "Being where over nine thousand people are buried shouldn't be easy."

"No." She fought wrapping her arms around him. Putting her arms around Caleb for any reason was a big no-no, but she longed to ease his obvious pain. "I'd say that I understand, because that's the first thing I want to say. But the truth is, as a civilian I'm not sure I can understand how being here feels to someone who served." She eyed his rigid stance and an awful thought swept over her, one that might have her hugging him yet. "Caleb, did you lose friends you served with?"

"Lose them?" He turned toward her, and she wished she could see his eyes from behind the shield of his sunglasses, but only her reflection shined back at her. "You mean, did any of the men and women I served with die in the line of duty?"

She knew the answer before he continued. The clenching of his jaw said it all.

"Yeah, Ivy, some of them died, a close friend of mine, specifically." Glancing back down at the tombstone, his shoulders lifted with the deep breath he sucked in. "I'd have taken Blake's place, any of their places, if that had been an option given to me."

Her heart ached for the things he'd seen and done, for the people he'd lost. Even beyond her grandfather, she'd cared for veterans during her residency, was familiar with the survivor's guilt so many of them felt when they'd survived skirmishes that others hadn't, was familiar with the post-traumatic stress symptoms so many experienced. That he'd lost a close friend—

Oh, Caleb.

"I'm sorry about your friend, and very glad you didn't die."

She may have just met him, but the world was a better place because he existed, a safer place.

She was sure of it. Giving in to whatever that warmth moving through her was, she placed her hand on his arm, hoping he understood what she didn't know how to express given the short time since they'd met.

How had it only been days when she felt as if she'd always known him?

How was it that touching him felt so right and yet as if she should jerk away her hand before it was branded by the feel of his skin beneath her fingertips?

Seeming to pull himself from wherever his thoughts had gone, he shifted his mirrored gaze to where her fingers pressed against his arm, then back up. Ivy dropped her hand to her side. She didn't drag her gaze from where he looked at her from behind those blasted sunglasses, though. She didn't feel as if she could.

After what felt like an eternity but couldn't have been more than a few seconds, he broke the contact. "I'm glad I didn't die, too. Sorry if I sounded as if that's not the case."

Thank God, because she couldn't imagine not having met him.

"Blake was a good guy. The best. Being here, it may sound crazy, but I swear that earlier, I felt his presence."

"It's a powerful place." She itched to touch him, to grasp his hand, but since he'd just pulled his arm free it felt weird to remake the connection.

"That it is."

Throat tight, Ivy stared at him in awe. Not just at who he was, but at how he affected her.

"What?" His brows drew together above his shades.

"You're a really nice guy, aren't you?"

Snorting, he shook his head. "For the record, being described as a really nice guy isn't the way a soldier wants to be known."

"I certainly didn't mean my words as an insult. Quite the opposite. But perhaps I should have said that you're a really good man, instead."

"Not always, but these days, I try to be."

Ivy's ever-present curiosity where he was concerned had her wanting him to elaborate, but his gaze shifted beyond her to where their group had moved far ahead.

"Come on, Doc. We need to catch up with our veterans."

"Smile, Doc." Caleb held up his phone to snap a photo of Ivy talking with two French reenactors at the Brevands memorial ceremony. Both men were in full "Filthy Thirteen" regalia with their hair shaved into mohawks and their faces painted like the First Demolition Section of the Regimental Headquarters Company of the 506th Parachute Infantry Regiment, 101st Airborne Division. The paratroopers had emulated the Native Americans in appearance and reportedly, yelled "Geronimo!" as they jumped. The "Filthy Thirteen" were also credited with liberating the French village and the town honored their legacy with the memorial and annual ceremony. Caleb and Ivy's veterans were part of today's events.

At his request, Ivy smiled. Caleb snapped the picture. Then the two reenactors, both around his and Ivy's ages, moved in for a posed shot with her sandwiched between them. Her smile was real, and Caleb felt a green twinge. He didn't like it but couldn't help but be aware of the sensation. He wasn't the jealous type, not even with Katrina. Other men hadn't been his ex's issue; his lack of interest in worldly goods had been what drove her away. But even if he were the jealous type, he sure didn't have any right to feel that way with Ivy.

"Your turn." She reached for his phone. "Get with them and I'll take one of you. Say, 'Eiffel Tower.'"

Caleb didn't hug up with the guys the way they'd done with her, but he smiled, then thanked them. The reenactors' English was limited, as was his and Ivy's French, but with patience and a little creativity they managed to have a decent conversation. A costumed, beautiful woman and young boy of around four, also in costume, joined them. One of the reenactors' eyes lit and he proudly introduced them as his wife and son.

More photos were taken, including one Ivy

snapped of the cute kid giving him a high five. Pure joy shone on her face. "*Merci.*"

The kid grinned.

When others joined them for photos with the reenactors, he and Ivy stepped back to give them room. They relocated to a monument, where Ivy motioned for him to stand next to the eagle with its wings spread and he did so.

"Oh, let me get one with both of you." Mary took Ivy's phone, then snapped a few shots of them next to the monument. She handed the phone back to Ivy. "Y'all look so good together."

Her cheeks going pink and not from the sunshine, Ivy averted her gaze. "Um, yeah, thanks for taking the photo, Mary."

The woman beamed at them a moment, then went back to where townspeople were swarming her father for autographs of his preprinted postcards.

"You'll have to text me copies of your photos."

"Sure." Ivy looked relieved that he hadn't directly commented on what Mary had said. "You'll have to do the same with the ones you've taken. Although, I've already taken so many that I've no idea when I'll have time to go through them."

"I hear you. I'm not normally one for taking many pictures, but you certainly wouldn't know that based on this trip." He had taken quite a few. More perhaps than he should have that featured Ivy. He assured himself that it was because they were both on the medical team and often paired together. He suspected it had more to do with the fact that he saw her in his mind even when he shut his eyes. As far as Mary's comment, well, he imagined any man would look better when standing next to a stunning woman like Ivy.

Soon it was time for the ceremony to begin. The Brevands mayor and a few other civil servants spoke. As flowers were being laid at the foot of the etched memorial stone, Caleb glanced toward Ivy. She appeared completely enthralled with what was happening. Her gaze was hidden behind her sunglasses, but she'd lifted her hand to her chest, as if powerfully moved by how the soldiers who'd freed the village were being remembered and honored.

Was she thinking about her great-grandfather? How she wished he were there, too? It was obvious she'd been close to him. She'd barely mentioned her parents other than the tourist trinkets, just her great-grandfather several times throughout the week. His gaze went to their veterans, then he leaned close to her ear and whispered, "Paul looks as if he's fallen asleep."

"He's almost a hundred. They'll forgive him." Frowning at his interrupting her viewing of the ceremony, she went back to watching.

Yeah, she was right. He needed to focus on what was being said and not be distracted by the lovely brunette at his side. That was pretty much how his trip was going. Be in awe of how grateful the French people of Normandy were and be in awe of Ivy McEwen. Emotions felt more intense in France.

After the ceremony ended, the crowd swarmed around the veterans for photos and to thank them. The men smiled, gave thumbs-up and handed out photo postcards.

Ivy smiled. "They're rock stars over here. You must be proud to have served."

His chest puffing with that pride, Caleb nodded. "It was my honor."

A soft smile played on her lips, drawing his gaze to her mouth. "Spoken like a true hero."

"That I'm not. Just a kid who grew up wanting to jump out of airplanes and shoot things. Joining the military let me do that without going to jail."

Her eyes widened and she gave a low laugh. "Well, when you put it that way…"

Staring at where the veterans greeted one local after another, Caleb shrugged. "Just telling you the truth."

One small part of it, but still, the truth.

Ivy eyed him. "So, when I can tell how much you loved being in the military, why aren't you still?"

"It's not because I don't want to be," he admitted. "My military career ended when I was medically discharged."

"You were hurt?" Horror darkened the blue

of her eyes as she stared into his, then her gaze skimmed over him, assessing for damage that she must have somehow missed. "Are you okay now? What happened?"

"I'm fine." Mostly. "I landed wrong during a jump." He'd leave off the reasons why he'd landed wrong and that he'd been lucky to land, to live, at all. Had that parachute been silk, it wouldn't have been fit for anything other than tattered rags. Just recalling those harrowing moments had him grimacing, but he forcibly relaxed his face and jaw.

"I'm glad you're okay." Her voice sounded overly emotional, causing him to study her and almost tell her more. That he wanted to tell her stunned him. There were some things he didn't discuss. Some things he hid behind the smile he kept ready on the surface. Life was good. He'd learned long ago he could focus on the good or the bad. He chose the good and did his best to forget the bad. Occasionally the nightmares refused to let him, but for the most part he was proud of how he survived day by day. But he didn't talk about it. Not to the therapist the army had arranged for him. Not with friends or family. Talking about it didn't help a thing. So the strong urge to say more to Ivy threw him off-kilter.

Not once during those long, painful days of recovery had he been tempted to tell Katrina that his internal pain far outweighed the physical. That Blake's death gutted him. Now, knowing that she'd only stepped back into his life because she'd thought he'd join the family business, he was glad he'd not been tempted.

So it made no sense that he'd want to tell Ivy how his best friend had died when their mission had been compromised and their plane had been shot down mere moments after they'd cleared it, that they'd both been hit by shrapnel, Caleb's leg. Blake's chute.

Her gaze bore into him, seeing things he'd always preferred no one see. Some things were better to keep to one's self. Caleb glanced at his watch, then the still-thick crowd near the reenactors they'd photographed with earlier. "What do you think? Should I let my hair grow out down the middle?"

He didn't look toward her. He didn't have to. His quick subject change said what he couldn't, but she let him get away with it.

"They're definitely impressive, aren't they?"

As was Ivy.

"Dr. Ivy!" Mary's voice rang out above the crowd. "Someone get Dr. Ivy."

Without looking his way, Ivy took off toward where Mary's voice had come from. Caleb followed close behind.

A heavy-set male who appeared to be in his late fifties slumped forward, gasping for air and clutching at his chest. *Gray* best described his skin color.

"What's going on?" Ivy asked, slipping her backpack off and swinging it around for easy access. Caleb followed suit.

"I was with dad, when this man said he didn't feel well," Mary began. "Next thing I knew, he sat down on the ground. He doesn't look so good."

"Thanks for your help, Mary. I need someone to call for emergency services and then if I can get you and the others to step back to give him room to breathe and us room to work, that would be great," Caleb assured the distressed woman.

"What's your name?" Ivy touched the man's shoulder, drawing his attention to her. When he continued to stare blankly at her, she tried again. *"Comment t'appelles-tu?"*

"Baptiste," the man said, wincing as he did so.

"Is there someone here who can translate for me?" Ivy asked, glancing around the gathering crowd. One of the reenactors stepped forward. "Ask him if he has a heart problem or is on any medications."

Caleb slipped his pulse oximeter onto the man's fingertip, then reached for his blood pressure cuff to check the man's pressure while Ivy and the interpreter continued to question the man. While talking, Ivy dug through her backpack, pulling out her medication bag.

"Tell Baptiste, this is nitroglycerin." She removed a bottle's lid and shook a tablet into the cap. "It's a tablet to increase the blood supply to the heart and decrease how hard the heart is having to work. I need him to put it in his mouth. He doesn't swallow it, he just needs to let the tablet sit beneath his tongue."

The interpreter told the in-pain man, who nodded and held out his hand. Ivy upturned the tablet into his palm and Baptiste put it in his mouth. Caleb held up the blood pressure cuff, showing Baptiste what he intended to do. The man nodded, then wincing, grabbed at his chest again.

Working fast, Caleb checked Baptiste's blood pressure. Or tried to. The cuff wasn't picking up a pressure. He looked at the pulse oximeter, watching as the number raced. "Pulse is bouncing around from the one-forties to the one-sixties."

Ivy gave a slight nod of acknowledgment.

Caleb had grabbed the defibrillator at the last moment, thinking he probably wouldn't need the equipment that took up a good chunk of his backpack. Unless emergency services arrived soon, he might well be glad he did.

"Baptiste, stay with me," Ivy said, tapping the man's cheek. "Look at me."

Baptiste had been sitting up but slumped over. Ivy and the interpreter laid him back on the grass.

"Pulse is over two hundred." Caleb wished they had oxygen as he opened the defibrillator.

He placed his mouth barrier guard close in case they needed to deliver breaths. "Get his shirt off."

"Here. Give me the razor." Ivy reached for the razor at the side of the defibrillator kit. "Those are never going to stick, otherwise."

With a few quick swipes, she shaved patches where Caleb needed to put the leads. As soon as she finished, he pressed the lead to the man's chest. Then waited as the machine read the man's rhythm.

"He's in ventricular fibrillation." He pulled the pulse oximeter off the man's finger. "All clear," he ordered.

Ivy leaned back, putting her hand out to keep the interpreter away from the man. "Don't touch him. Not anywhere."

The second no one was touching Baptiste, Caleb pressed the button to deliver the shock that would hopefully put Baptiste's heart back in rhythm. The man's body jerked, and Caleb held his breath as he watched the defibrillator's screen.

"It didn't work." Ivy moved over the patient. "I'm starting compressions. Keep a check on his breathing. Give breaths if needed."

Caleb slipped the pulse oximeter back onto Baptiste's finger; oxygenation was in the eighties. "You still have that extra epinephrine from the plane in your backpack?"

She rhythmically compressed his chest. "It's there."

He grabbed her bag, found her liquids bag and pulled out the vial of epinephrine. He gathered a syringe, alcohol swab, and set them aside. He hoped they got a rhythm restored to where they didn't need the medication. If they didn't have Baptiste's heart out of the rapid quivering within a few minutes, he'd inject it.

"Caleb, deliver breaths. He's quit breathing."

He let loose with a low curse, ripping open the cellophane covering on the mouth barrier that would protect him and Baptiste from pathogens. He gave two breaths, then glanced toward the defibrillator, making sure it wasn't recommending another shock yet.

"Not yet," Ivy said, apparently also keeping a check on the screen. They worked together, her compressing, him delivering breaths.

"Swap with me," Caleb suggested, knowing her arms had to be jelly at this point.

She didn't argue, just quickly exchanged positions with him.

"Time to deliver another charge." He moved back, waited until she'd also done so.

"All clear," she said. "If this doesn't restore rhythm, I'm giving the epi."

"Understood. All clear." He pressed the button, causing Baptiste's body to jerk.

"Come on," Ivy told the machine as they waited to see if the electric charge knocked Baptiste's heart out of the dangerous rhythm. "Come on."

"Yes!" He reached out to high-five her when the screen no longer showed ventricular fibrillation.

Baptiste didn't open his eyes. But gasped, then coughed.

They monitored him closely, ready to restart cardiopulmonary resuscitation if needed. Baptiste didn't regain consciousness, but he continued to breathe on his own and, although his rhythm was irregular, it wasn't the dangerous initial one.

"The *Les secours* is here," the interpreter told them as a uniformed duo joined them.

After Baptiste was on his way to the hospital, Caleb grinned at the brunette who was knelt next to Roy, chatting with him.

She glanced up, caught him watching her and grinned. "What?"

"Looks like you saved the day again," he praised.

She stared into his eyes a moment, wild emotion swirling in her blue depths. "Looked more like *we* saved the day again to me. We make a good team."

CHAPTER SEVEN

LATER THAT DAY, a local attorney had everyone from the SMVF to his home for a late lunch. The estate ran as a bed-and-breakfast with a gorgeous event room. Red, white and blue decorations and small flags on the tables gave a festive, patriotic look. Caleb and Ivy ended up at different tables, but she was in his direct line of vision. It might have been better if she hadn't been, though. He was having trouble staying focused on what Roy said. Seemed as if he was having trouble focusing period. While taking care of Baptiste, he and Ivy had worked seamlessly. They made a good team, she'd said. He'd not thought in terms of being a team with a woman since Katrina. The first time, he'd been young, a mere high school kid at an expensive prep school his parents had hoped would steer him in a nonmilitary direction. The second, he'd been hospitalized and she'd been a welcome distraction from his misery. It hadn't taken long for her to leave him again when she realized he'd had no plans to join the rest of his family at the shipping business. A broken man who could have had a great life as part of a power couple with her but chose to wallow in his misery instead, she'd accused. He had grieved Blake's death, grieved his medical discharge from the career he loved, but "wallow" had been harsh. He'd just been driven to get back on his feet, literally.

"She's a looker, isn't she?" Roy interrupted Caleb's meanderings.

"Who?" Caleb shifted his gaze to the grinning older man, took a sip of his water and pretended complete ignorance, as if Roy hadn't just caught him staring at the woman who'd said they made a great team. *As a couple* had been a long way from what she'd meant, but it was no secret he was attracted to her, hence Roy's incoming comments.

"You know who." Roy chuckled. "If I was younger, I'd give you a run for your money."

"You and Owen, but for the record, I'm not sure I'm in the running." He wanted to be, though. He sure hadn't thought about meeting anyone when he'd agreed to go on this trip. He'd have laughed if Stan had suggested anything of the sort. Ivy made him curious to know more and uncover the many layers of who she was. She was different from anyone he'd ever met. Or maybe it was just the way he responded to her that was different from anyone else. Ivy was beautiful, inside and out from the best he could tell, but he'd met good people before and not been drawn to them like the proverbial moth to the flame.

In a different day and time, he'd have made moves on her, charmed her, had his way with her. Since Katrina's last reminder of why relationships were a bad idea following his accident, he rarely dated. But he was interested in Ivy. He sensed her interest, and her hesitation. Wooing her tempted, but there was an inherent fragility beneath her tough exterior that gave him his own hesitations. She'd obviously been hurt in the past. Who hadn't been these days? But he sure didn't want to be the guy who added to someone's pain, and Katrina had nailed home that was all he was good for since his heart belonged to the military and everything, everyone, would always take a distant second place.

"Sure, you aren't." Roy's wrinkled face brightened with merriment as he cackled. "Good thing you've got a week left to admit the truth to yourself and to her. Youth is wasted on the young."

"Yes, sir," Caleb agreed. He'd sure taken jumping for granted right up until his ankle shattered. Maybe Katrina had been right in that he was a broken man. He'd not viewed himself as whole since waking up in a military hospital and realizing the extent of his injuries, that he'd likely never qualify as a paratrooper again. Sometimes he dreamed, though.

"When you get to my age you've learned a

thing or two. One of those things is not wasting time on silly games," Roy continued. "Time is short. Don't be a dunce."

"You think I'm playing a silly game with Dr. McEwen?" Maybe he should take better advantage of the time they'd been given together. He'd not even thought of dating since Katrina. Now, with Ivy, his body reminded him he was a healthy male. He'd thought himself through with relationships. Did meeting Ivy change that or was it just that they were two healthy adults who found each other attractive and were in forced proximity?

"Game that's older than time." Roy grinned. "I've watched it a hundred times during my life. I always wonder why people do that and waste so much precious time. I've seen how you watch her. So has she, for that matter. You make her nervous, but in a good kind of way. Back in my day, we'd have at least asked to hold her hand by this point."

Mary, who was sitting opposite her father and had been in deep conversation with a French couple, was now curiously listening in to what her father said and nodding in agreement. Caleb was beginning to feel cornered and natural instinct had his fight or flight kicking in big-time.

"By this point? You realize I just met her a week ago, right?" Caleb reminded. But perhaps Roy was on to something. Maybe Caleb was overthinking everything where Ivy was concerned.

Maybe he needed to just put everything that had happened with Katrina in the past where it belonged. Ivy was nothing like worldly Katrina, who had cared more about his parents' wealth than she had about Caleb. Even if he was on board, Ivy might not be. He could see her response going either way and that might be part of his hesitation. Which was interesting as he'd never let the risk of failure stop him in the past. How often had he jumped that the odds weren't in his favor and yet he'd never paused? What held him back? Would Ivy even care that being a soldier mattered more to him than anything? And that now, peace mattered more than his bank account?

"A week? That long ago already? You're slacking, kid." Roy reached out and patted his hand. "Take it from an old coot, that girl is something special."

Hadn't Caleb thought the same thing? That he'd never met anyone like her? His gaze went back to where Ivy was laughing at something Owen was telling her. Her long hair was pulled back into a ponytail and pink tinged her high cheekbones. There was no telling what Owen had said. The man might be close to a hundred, but he was an incurable flirt.

And Ivy was something special.

After they'd eaten their delicious lunch, including more fresh baked bread that he was quickly becoming accustomed to having at each meal, they moved outdoors to enjoy the beautiful weather. Along with a few others, Caleb helped carry out chairs.

When they'd finished, he looked around for Ivy, spotting her heading down a gravel road.

"She asked Lara to keep an eye on the guys, saying she needed to walk off some of her lunch. If you hurry, you can catch her." Had Mary overheard all of what her father had been saying earlier?

Since stretching his legs would feel good, Caleb jogged to catch up with Ivy. It didn't take long. She'd paused to snap photos of an old outbuilding that had gorgeous roses growing near it.

"Want one with you in it?" he offered, wanting to be helpful and give himself a reason for joining her walk.

"I'm good." She slid her phone into her pocket. "Thanks, though."

"What if I'd like one?"

Seeming surprised, she shrugged. "Okay, pose and I'd be happy to take one."

Not what he'd meant, but Caleb went with it, handing his phone to Ivy, then giving her a cheesy smile.

"Here." She handed back his phone. "Check to make sure you like it."

Rather than check the photo, Caleb hit his camera icon, then leaned in next to Ivy for a selfie. "Say cheese."

Rather than look at the camera she stared at him in surprise. He snapped a photo. Shrugging, she glanced up, smiled and said, "Eiffel Tower."

Caleb took a few shots. "So much better than saying cheese. Have you been?"

She shook her head. "Not yet. I'm hoping there's time on the day we travel back to Paris."

Caleb hoped so, too. Seeing the iconic tower hadn't been on his radar but now, seeing it with Ivy ranked up there. Her eyes would sparkle more magnificently than the tower ever could.

There really must be something about France. He wasn't the kind of guy who went around thinking about how a woman's eyes would sparkle. The French must put something in their water. Or maybe it was all the delicious bread that made a person view things differently. Apparently, life just got all rose-colored glasses when you were drinking fine wine and eating fresh-baked bread.

Gravel crunched beneath their feet as they resumed their walk toward the pastures. There was a slight breeze that rustled the lush green trees lining the country road. A cow bellowed in the distance. If Caleb had been searching for peace, this moment was it: a full belly, beautiful surroundings and with a great person.

"Hope you don't mind me joining you," he told her, then patted his stomach. "With all the bread I'm eating, I needed to move. I may be bigger than a house by the time we go home."

"Yeah, I don't think you have anything to worry about with how fit you are." Her gaze dropped to his midsection, then, realizing what she'd done, she looked away. "I mean, um, oh, never mind."

Pleased with her compliment, Caleb couldn't resist teasing. "You think I'm fit?"

"You have to remember that I've been hanging out with men who are knocking a hundred. It's all in one's perspective."

He laughed at her quick-witted comment. "And here I thought you were giving me a compliment."

"I was, not that you need compliments to know that you take care of your body. It's obvious that you do. You go for a run in the mornings before I've awakened."

He wouldn't be winning any marathons with his jogs, but he strove to keep his legs strong by his exercise and stretching regime. "Then, thank you for the compliment. I'm glad you noticed."

Ignoring his comment, she pointed down the gravel road that ran deeper into the farm "Let's walk to where those horses are near that fence. My great-grandfather's farm has a section with fences like those made from cut trees and I want to see them up close."

"Did he have horses?"

"Not for years. Actually, he hasn't had any animals in years other than ones that belong to others. In his late eighties, he sold his cattle and most of his farm equipment and started leasing the land out to one of his neighbors." Ivy glanced his way. "He left me his farm."

"You going to take up farming?"

"For now, I'm hoping his neighbor will continue to lease the land. There are a lot of things I have to figure out after I get settled in Knoxville. I'd barely finished residency prior to our leaving on this trip."

"Are you planning to live at the farm?"

She nodded. "It's what I'd always planned to do. I'd just planned on Gramps being there with me."

"He will be. In your heart and your mind."

Ivy's gaze cut to him and she smiled. "He's always there. Always."

Caleb loved his family, but he was the black sheep by not following in his parents' corporate footsteps. What would it have been like to have someone who he felt such a connection with? "Tell me about him."

Ivy looked shocked at his request. "You want to hear about my great-grandfather? Luke couldn't stand me to talk about him."

"I'm not Luke."

"Thank God. I stayed with that man longer than I should have."

"I'd like to hear about why you did that, too, but that's a conversation for a different day. It's much too beautiful a day to ruin it by talking about someone who makes your nose curl that way."

Relaxing her face, she nodded. "You're right. It is. I'd much rather talk about Gramps."

"What's your favorite memory of him?"

"I have lots of great memories so it's difficult to pick just one. He'd take me out on his tractor with him, we'd fish in his pond, but maybe my favorite was watching him with my great-grandmother before she died. They made being in love look like so much fun. I wanted that so badly that I settled for less. That's why I've put conditions on any future relationship."

"Conditions?"

"Things that I hope will increase odds of any future relationship's success."

Curious, he wanted to know more, but she was so relaxed talking about her great-grandfather that he didn't want to risk her clamming up on him.

"So Gramps was your great-grandfather? What happened to your grandparents?"

"My grandmother died giving birth to my mother. My grandmother was Gramps and Grammie's only child. They were devastated. Mom says they never forgave her for being born. I'm not sure I believe that, but she and Gramps never jibed, not the way we did."

"I'm sorry. Is that why he left the farm to you?"

"Mom would have sold it. He knew that."

"And that you wouldn't?"

"I loved the farm."

"Then he left it to the right person."

As they meandered toward the fence, Ivy told him stories of her great-grandfather's farm. Of how the ninety-eight-year-old man had rarely sat down at any point in his life, having come back from the war, married her grandmother and lived life to the fullest.

"Like the guys here, Gramps never sat down. I think that's why he did so well, why Owen and these guys do so well. They've stayed active."

Caleb was all for following in their footsteps. He hoped he never had a reason to sit down and stay down.

Not ever again.

The months following his accident had been the roughest point in his life. Maybe that's why he'd allowed Katrina back into his life. He'd been desperate for any connection outside the rehabilitation facility. She'd accused him of being like a trapped animal. That's how he'd felt. Trapped. By his own body's limitations.

Staying committed to taking care of his body wasn't difficult when he recalled how miserable he'd been laid up and dependent upon others for the simplest things.

A waste of air. That was what Katrina had said.

You should have done your family a favor and died when that plane went down.

He might not have the relationship with them that Ivy had had with her great-grandfather, but they hadn't wanted him to die. They'd just been too busy working to come around much while he was healing. Not that he'd wanted them or anyone to see him that way. Maybe that was why he'd let Katrina come back, because ultimately, he'd known she'd leave because she'd never settle for his footloose and fancy-free lifestyle.

Glancing at the woman leaning against the fence, petting a mare who'd come over to check them out probably hoping for a treat, Caleb wondered at Ivy. He was a minimalist with no real roots. Her roots ran deep on a Tennessee farm.

He was attracted to her, wanted to date her, but she was looking for what her great-grandparents had had. She deserved that. Until his accident, Caleb had never stayed in one place long during his adult life. He likely wouldn't have stayed in Knoxville if not for Blake's widow needing his help with TransCare. Now he didn't know what his future held. He was content, and yet, he wasn't. He blamed his inability to jump, but perhaps it was more than that.

"You're very quiet." Still stroking her hands over the horse's neck, Ivy glanced toward him. "Have I bored you with all my talk about Gramps and the farm?"

He shook his head. "You could read an old phone book and I don't think I'd be bored, not with how expressive your face gets."

"Yeah, well, if I was reading an old phone book, the expression on my face would be boredom, so nothing exciting about that."

It really didn't matter what she was saying. It was Ivy herself that was exciting, being near her, reveling in the electric vibes she sent through him, wondering what she'd say or do next.

"This may sound cheesy, but I don't think I could ever be bored when looking at your face no matter your expression."

She eyed him suspiciously, then laughing nervously, turned back to love on the horse. He suspected she didn't know what to say. He understood. He didn't, either, because what he said was true and he'd only known her less than a week.

"I think you were supposed to turn back there," Ivy pointed out when Caleb drove past a road on the turnabout. Turnabouts were apparently a big thing in this area, because they'd come upon several of them during the trip. Ivy found them confusing as did her phone's GPS system, obviously.

These days, she found a lot of things confusing, especially in regard to Caleb. Since the prior day when he'd made his cheesy remark about her face, she'd been able to think of little else.

"You're sure?" He glanced toward her. "I

looked at the directions earlier, and I think we're on the correct road."

She studied her phone map, then looked back at where they were. "According to my phone's GPS, that was our turn."

"No problem. The directions I'd looked at earlier had routed us a different way, but I imagine that there's more than one way to get there. We'll take your phone's directions." Caleb circled the car around the turnabout, then exited at where she indicated.

"We can always backtrack if my GPS leads us astray." Hopefully, it wouldn't. They weren't in a time crunch, but she didn't want to take away from their seeing as many iconic places as possible during their free afternoon. Pointe du Hoc wasn't on the veterans' itinerary, so needed to be visited during downtime. When Phillipe had offered his car, they'd jumped at the opportunity to explore some of the iconic spots along the coastline.

Caleb strummed his fingers against the steering wheel. "Do you know the history behind Pointe du Hoc?"

"It's where army rangers scaled hundred-foot cliffs to take out artillery that could fire upon Omaha and Utah Beaches on D-Day."

Caleb looked impressed. "I've met well-seasoned soldiers who don't know about Point du

Hoc or what happened there. Did you study up for this trip?"

"I've been studying for this trip my whole life." She laughed. "I was forever asking my Gramps questions. As a child, I didn't realize I was asking about things he didn't talk about, but for whatever reason, with me, he did and I soaked up every word."

"That was probably cathartic for him. At least, that's what the therapist I was forced to see told me. That talking about the things that I'd seen and done was good for me. I'd say talking to you helped him heal."

Ivy's heart warmed at Caleb's comment while simultaneously clenching that he'd seen and done things requiring him to see a therapist. No doubt the military had required it after his friend had died. She couldn't imagine the heartbreak that he must have felt to have been there and survived when his friend hadn't. "That's a wonderful thought and I hope I helped him find peace. That's what this trip is supposed to do for the veterans, to help them find peace. Regardless, Gramps never seemed to mind my questions and I asked him lots because I was fascinated by his military history. His WWII service was a bond we shared."

"My love of the military was an oddity in my family, so your relationship with him sounds idyllic to me. So you shared WWII history and the Tennessee Volunteers?"

"We kept up with the team together, just as we kept up with anything and everything that would come out about World War II. When a new movie or documentary would air, we planned ahead for me to visit so we could watch it together if it was at all possible. I grew up in Nashville, so just a few hours from Gramps. He'd drill me on the accuracy, so I had to know my stuff." She smiled at the memories running through her head. "As I advanced in school, watching together became more difficult with life commitments, so we'd watch, then discuss over the phone."

"You're lucky to have had such a close relationship with your great-grandfather. My family had no military interest. My brother attended my basic training graduation, but none of my family understood my passion for my career. Does it sound terrible if I admit I'm jealous of your great-grandfather?"

Ivy hated his lack of support and wondered why his family hadn't been there for him. She'd been lucky to be so loved.

"It doesn't sound terrible. Everyone should be envious of Gramps. He was the best, so I totally understand why someone would want our relationship. It was enviable," she admitted. "I was blessed to have him for so many years in my life and should have found a way to see him more, you know? Med school and residency could have waited." Grief and guilt hitting, she closed her eyes. "They would have waited if I'd known I was going to lose him."

"Everyone dies eventually and he lived a good, long life. It sounds as if you had a great relationship, and he knew you loved him. That's what is important."

"Gramps knew I loved him." She repeated his claim, her words choking her. She cleared her throat. "What about you? Are you close with your family?" She really wanted to know more, to know why only his brother had been at Caleb's graduation from Basic. "Was there someone in the service who influenced your desire to be in the military?"

"No one in the military that they're aware of, although I think most Americans had at least one extended family member drafted for one of the World Wars."

"No direct military family members, but one day you decided you wanted to join the army?" she pressed. "How did that happen?"

"I always wanted to be in the army. I liked playing with those little green plastic men and watching war movies. Maybe that was what influenced me."

"Did the toy company make those army men with parachutes?" Ivy teased, trying to picture him as a child playing with the toys. It was difficult to imagine Caleb as anything other than the virile man sitting in the driver's seat.

"Those only came in the fancier sets." He grinned. "What about you? With your obvious love and appreciation for the military, what kept you from enlisting? You could have pursued medicine in the military."

"At one point in time, I considered," she admitted. "But that would have meant having to fly and we know how I feel about that." She wrinkled her nose with displeasure. "Even Gramps agreed that I shouldn't enlist."

"What did he want you to do?"

Ivy's heart swelled as she recalled the conversation with her great-grandfather. "To be happy."

Caleb cut his gaze toward her. "That's it? He didn't have a preconceived idea that he tried to force upon you of what would make you happy? Didn't try to push you to go into the family business?"

"Our family business would be farming, I guess, and he never tried to push me to do that. I enjoyed being with him on the farm, but it wasn't my calling. He was pleased when I told him I planned to follow in my great-grandmother's footsteps and become a doctor. I'm named after her and he thought it perfect that I carry on her love of helping others. He said he always thought that's what I should do but hadn't wanted to influence my decision."

"I'm sure he was proud of you. Going to medical school is hard work."

"Tell me about it. Oh, turn left up here." She pointed at an upcoming road. "There were days when I wondered if I'd get through med school."

"I can't see you quitting something you started. You seem like a very determined person who keeps pushing forward."

Even when she should just admit she was wrong. She should have called it quits with Luke eons before she did.

"You're right. I'd never have dropped out of school and let him, or myself, see me as a failure. I wouldn't have dishonored my great-grandmother's legacy that way." Her relationship with Luke had been a dishonor. How many of her "friends" had known he was cheating, but had failed to tell her? Had they all been laughing behind her back?

"Her name was Ivy, too?"

"No, but my middle name is Rose. My great-grandfather always said she was the prettiest flower in the garden and that's why he picked her."

Slowing the car to make the turn, Caleb glanced her way. "Then, you carry on her legacy in more ways than one."

Caleb's compliment had Ivy's heart thudding hard against her rib cage. Ha! Everything about Caleb made her pulse pound. Including the fact that he'd taken the route she'd recommended even though it was different from the one he'd intended. It had already taken them ten minutes longer than the time frame he'd given when they'd left the bed-and-breakfast at Sainte-Mère-église, but he'd not said one negative word or pointed out that his way was better. The contrast to Luke couldn't be more stark. Why had she stayed in that relationship so long when there were men like Caleb out in the world?

Not that she was in a relationship with Caleb, just...just, maybe she wanted to be. Yes, they were in a magical bubble of spending two weeks away from their "real" lives, but there was something about him that was different from any man she'd ever known. Not true. He reminded her of her favorite qualities in Gramps. The qualities she'd thought the current generation lacked, but that she found so attractive and had hoped to someday find. Face heating, she knew she needed to get her thoughts under control and refocused on the matter at hand, which was getting them to their destination.

But the past had taught her that dating a man who wasn't her economic equal would eventually lead to problems. Problems she could avoid by only becoming involved with men who wouldn't be threatened by her independence.

"Pointe du Hoc is only about four miles from Utah Beach, right?" She needed a subject change because she wasn't ready to delve into what Caleb had meant by his sweet comment. Had he been implying that he found her the prettiest flower in the garden and planned to pick her? And, if that's what he meant, what was she going to do about it? Go with it to see what happened or set him straight that she wasn't in the market for another heartbreak? That they were in an environment that forced togetherness, but back in the real world, he'd see her in a different, less flattering, light. "We're getting close."

Not taking his gaze from the road, he nodded. "This was one of my top places to visit."

"It was great of Phillipe and Delphine to let us use their car." See, she could make normal conversation even when he'd made cheesy compliments two days in a row.

"The people of Normandy are impressive in their hospitality." He tapped his thumbs against the steering wheel, matching beat with the crazy pounding in her chest.

"With your history as a paratrooper and all the airborne history in the area, I'm surprised that Pointe du Hoc made your top list."

He shrugged. "Just because I was a paratrooper doesn't mean that I can't appreciate what the rangers accomplished here. Those brave men deserve to be remembered. All the soldiers from D-Day do."

"Agreed." She pointed to a sign. "There's our turn."

They parked and walked the short distance to the entrance. The cliffs were hauntingly beautiful as they jutted above the coastline. The wind whipped at Ivy, loosening hair strands from her ponytail and dancing them about her head in defiance of her repeated attempts to recapture them. Despite the summer heat, the breeze carried a chill, perhaps as a reminder of the past. Ivy rubbed her arms.

"The wind cuts right into you, doesn't it?" Caleb asked as they made their way toward steps that led into an old bunker.

She crammed her hands into her pockets. "Yes, but I'm not going to complain. Not here about something as insignificant as the wind being cold."

His gaze met hers. "Perhaps here is the best place to say how you're feeling. The freedom to speak your mind is one of the things those men were fighting for."

Again, awed by his insight, Ivy studied him. "True, but you aren't going to hear me complain."

The corner of his mouth lifted. "I wouldn't expect to. You're much more a grit-your-teeth-and-bear-it kind of person."

Ivy couldn't argue. She would much rather just suck it up and deal than to verbalize negativity. Complaining sure didn't change anything. Gramps had always told her that if she didn't like something, to do something to make it better. For the most part, she felt that was what she did in life. Where she'd failed was when it came to relationships. For whatever reasons, she'd turned a blind eye to things she didn't want to acknowledge. Delaying the inevitable rarely proved beneficial. Today's nippy wind was nothing in the grand scheme of life.

They went through an old bunker, peering out the slit windows that looked out to the sea, then moved back to the path where they marveled at the many craterous land indentions made by bombings that had occurred so long ago. They took in the sights, the smells of the ocean, the continued whipping of the wind, the heaviness of the knowledge of what had taken place as the rangers took out enemy forces to protect their comrades landing at Utah and Omaha Beaches. While all that had been going on, Gramps had been jumping near Sainte-Mère-église with his company in the Eighty-Second.

Ivy stumbled on her way down a set of steps. "Oops."

Caleb grasped hold of her hand, making sure she stayed upright. Electricity shot over her skin, prickling her flesh, and almost made her lose balance again. His fingers were warm and strong as they clasped with hers and didn't let go.

"You okay?" Concern shone on his face.

"Fine." Why hadn't she pulled her hand free? Why, instead, were their fingers still clasped as they made their way through the bunker? Why was she still holding his hand fifteen minutes later as they made their way through the memorial area with its placards denoting different brave men who'd taken Pointe du Hoc? Why did the heat of his skin eradicate the wind's chill? Whatever it was, having her fingers laced with his made her feel better, as if he could protect her from even the elements. How silly was she that she was marveling at their held hands rather than putting a quick end to his presumptuousness?

Was it presumptuous when she liked his hand holding hers and she hadn't pulled away? She obviously didn't mind too much, or she wouldn't allow him to do so as they continued to make their way along the pathway overlooking the sea far below and back toward the park's exit.

After they'd left and were heading to find somewhere to eat, they passed a beautiful building with ivy growing up the side, she pulled out her phone to take photos along their drive back.

A thought hit and disappointment gripped her belly. "Oh, no! We forgot to take any pictures."

Caleb's amber eyes shifted toward her, connecting and mesmerizing with their intensity. "We've not gone that far and we can go back if you want to take a few, but I don't need pictures to remember today. Visiting Pointe du Hoc was unforgettable, don't you think?"

Ivy's breath caught. He was right. Their visit had been unforgettable.

Just as she suspected the man sitting next to her was going to prove unforgettable.

CHAPTER EIGHT

IVY PAUSED TO peer into a shop window along the cobbled street running between the colorful buildings in Le Vieux Bassin at the Honfleur harbor. "Stopping for an early dinner in this gorgeous town was a wonderful idea."

"I wasn't necessarily thinking about buying our meal from a street vendor, but I enjoyed the sunshine and watching the boats."

"I can't imagine it being more delicious if we'd sat down at a five-star restaurant. My mackerel was yummy."

"Mine, too." A couple walked past them, eating ice cream cones. Caleb glanced her way and waggled his brows. "What do you think? There's always room for ice cream."

Glancing his way, she shook her head. "You think I'm going to trust you when it comes to dessert? I think not after you convinced me to try *crottes de mouettes*."

His eyes twinkled with mischief. "You looked as if you were enjoying them."

"Right up until you told me they were seagull droppings," she muttered.

Caleb chuckled. "I'm not sure why they're called that, since they're just a candy made of caramel and chocolate, but your face was priceless when I told you."

"Priceless?" She rolled her eyes. "Ha ha. I mean, I thought you were just teasing, but we are in a foreign country. Dietary habits are different, so I did wonder for a second."

"They were just candy." His lips twitched. "At least, as far as I know, they were. My French leaves a lot to be desired, so anything's possible."

She poked him in the ribs. "Stop. You're ruining how good those tasted."

He grinned. "We should talk about what they make their ice cream from."

She put her hands over her ears. "La-la-la… I can't hear you."

He laughed. "Milk."

"You're bad," The smile on her face undermined her comment. "Come on. Let's go in this shop. Maybe you can find more key chains, because I'm sure the hundreds you've already bought aren't nearly enough."

"I may have to buy an extra suitcase to carry them home," he teased as they went into the shop.

"Are you a habitual key chain giver?" she accused when he made a beeline for the shop's souvenir trinkets.

"Not really. Most of my past travels had to do with deployment or military assignments." Picking up a key chain, then putting it back, he turned to her. "I hadn't really thought about it, but this is my first time traveling since returning to civilian life."

The emotion in his voice had her heart squeezing. "Why key chains?"

He shrugged. "Why not key chains?"

"Just trying to understand if there's any symbolism to the key chains. I mean, are you trying to give your friends and family the key to the world or is there some deeper meaning?"

Rather than laugh, his forehead scrunched. "It's just a key chain, Ivy. Nothing more."

But something about his tone made her wonder if she hadn't hit a sensitive spot, perhaps one he hadn't even realized he had.

"Well, if they have one with a photo of these gorgeous buildings along the inner harbor, I may have to get one."

He arched a brow. "You? Buy a souvenir?"

"Shocking, I know." She followed him out of the shop, taking in the beauty of where they were with the gorgeous boats in the harbor, red-canopied vendors along the cobblestoned streets and the multicolored buildings. "Maybe I should just take some pictures. I still can't believe I forgot to take any while we were at Pointe du Hoc."

"I offered to return." Side by side, they walked down the street.

"I know and I appreciate that, but I didn't want you to have to turn around just to take pictures. You were right when you said it was an unforgettable day."

"Not just at Pointe du Hoc."

She glanced his way, met his gaze, and her breath caught. He meant now because they'd spent the day together. She couldn't disagree. Their afternoon strolling along the inner harbor, looking at the boats, watching the waves come in along the beach, popping in and out of shops, then eating at the delicious street vendor, had been relaxing. A perfect date.

Only it wasn't a date.

"Ivy, I…" He hesitated, then seemed to change his mind on whatever he was going to say. "Hand me your phone and I'll take your photo with the harbor in the background."

Wondering what he'd started to say, she passed him her phone and smiled as he snapped pictures.

"Would you like me to take a photo of you together?" a woman with an American accent asked just as Caleb handed her phone back.

"That would be great." Ivy grabbed Caleb's hand and pulled him to where they could take a photo with the picturesque harbor in the background.

She didn't look at him, just held on to his hand as she smiled while the woman took a few shots.

"Get closer together," the woman encouraged, snapping another photo. "Now do something funny."

Ivy contorted her face, then realizing Caleb had given her bunny ears, frowned. "Hey!"

She grabbed at his fingers to pull them down, but, laughing, he held them higher than she could reach.

"Oh, these are great," their photographer praised, laughing at their antics, then handing Ivy's phone back. "How fun. You guys have a great rest of your trip. How much longer are you guys here?"

"About a week."

They said goodbye, then continued through the town, stopping to window-shop from time to time, and just soaking in the relaxed atmosphere of the quaint town.

"Let's ride the Ferris wheel."

Her spur-of-the-moment suggestion surprised her almost as much as it did Caleb.

"What about your fear of heights?"

"I don't have a fear of heights. I have a fear of flying," she clarified. "There's a difference."

"Okay. If you want to ride the Ferris wheel, we'll ride the Ferris wheel."

"You don't think I'm silly for wanting to ride it?"

He studied her a moment, then shook his head. "I think you're perfect because you want to ride it."

His praise did funny things to her insides, like make her breathy and feel as if she might float away. "And if I said I want to ride the carousel, too?"

"I'd say, you're in luck. I like carousels."

They rode the carousel first, choosing galloping horses next to each other. Feeling giddy, childlike even, she glanced Caleb's way, met his gaze, and he winked. Okay, there went feeling childish, because his wink made her feel very much womanly.

When the ride finished, he dismounted, then mock bowed and held out his hand. "My lady."

His lady. Ivy's breath caught. She could get off the horse just fine, but she placed her hand in his, let him assist her. She slid a leg around to where she could step down, but Caleb's hands went to her waist, lifting her. Rather than putting her on the ground, he held her, his hands burning through the cotton of her T-shirt. Ivy swallowed, keeping her eyes locked with his as he slowly lowered her, their bodies brushing as he did so. Fire shot through her at the contact. *Fire* because there was no other way to describe his touch.

Desire flickered in his eyes and Ivy sucked in a breath, reminding herself they were in a very public place, even though the emotions hitting her were all of the private variety. "Caleb?"

"Hmm?" His hand grasped hers, giving a gentle squeeze.

"I like carousels, too."

His amber eyes burning into her, he grinned. "Ready for the Ferris wheel, Doc?"

The following day, the town of Carentan hosted a ceremony at Cabbage Square attended by government and military officials from numerous countries. A massive canopy tent had been set up to keep the veterans out of the sunshine as the "distinguished" speakers reminded of why everyone was gathered there, celebrating France's liberation and continued freedom. A community center was set up for lunch and to rest prior to a parade. That evening, there was another meal and ceremony followed by a dance.

Throughout the day, Ivy stayed close to her veterans. All the WWII veterans from SMVF and the other veteran group were honored again during the meal that represented French, British, American and German cuisines. The sport's complex had been decorated with red, white and blue streamers draped from the ceiling, giving it a festive look. Veterans, the veteran association groups, dignitaries and current military there for various events were all present.

Caleb set his plate down on the table next to hers.

"Hungry?" she teased. Ivy had limited her choices to small helpings of two items representing each country. Caleb's plate appeared to have healthy samplings of every item offered.

"Starved."

Had she not met his gaze, she might not have thought anything about the exchange, but his look had her gulping. Did he feel as confused by their hand-holding as she did?

She was confused, all right. Confused over her own thoughts, emotions, and her own silly fantasies of meeting a man like Gramps.

Today, they'd been friendly, but he hadn't reached for her hand or given any indication that he'd held her hand the evening before.

Because his holding your hand was innocent and you're being silly, reading too much into an innocent gesture. Just stop.

Only, Ivy didn't buy it. There had been nothing innocent about his touch. Not on either of their parts. Holding hands might be a common gesture, but for them, it had been a big deal.

She ate most of her food. Caleb cleaned his plate. Where did he put all he ate?

Ivy's veterans claimed they were tired, so their host families left with them, rather than stay for the dance. Ivy would have been great with leaving, as well, but Phillipe and Delphine had commented on how much they looked forward to the dance each year. As Ivy and Caleb had ridden with them, they were left at the table watching the others. People of all ages, including a few of the hundred-plus-year-old veterans from the other group, danced and laughed.

"That's how I want to be," Caleb mused from beside her. He'd donned khaki slacks and a navy button-down that he'd rolled the sleeves up enough to reveal his smartwatch and tan forearms sprinkled with dark hair. In all her life Ivy couldn't recall finding a man's hands and wrists sexy, but Caleb Rivers's had her wishing she could fan herself. Okay, lots about him had her insides warm. Like the way he almost always had a smile and treated everyone in their group with genuine kindness and respect. Her gaze lingered on his hand. The one that had held hers. Something so simple and yet, his having held her hand had freed some complex reactions. She couldn't deny her interest. He appealed to everything inside her except for her logic. That part of her advised her to run as quickly as she could.

Wearing the one dress she'd brought with her, a simple red number that fell to just above her knees and that she'd even matched with red lipstick to pull the look together, Ivy gazed into his sunshine-hitting honey eyes. "How is it that you want to be?"

"Laughing and dancing until my dying day," he clarified. "They're having the time of their lives right here where so many of them could have lost their lives. They're enjoying the moment without worrying about the past or their limited future. They're truly living in the present. That's a marvelous place to be."

Looking toward the dance floor, her gaze landed upon a veteran who seemed to be especially enjoying himself as he held on to a younger woman's hands. Ivy couldn't help but smile at how happy he looked. A memory from her early childhood hit of Gramps grabbing her great-grandmother at the waist and spinning her around the kitchen, causing her to giggle. They'd pulled her in to join their happy carousing. Their love and joy for each other had been so obvious even through her childish eyes.

She'd thought she'd eventually marry Luke and raise their children at the farm she loved while practicing medicine in Knoxville. She never settled in her professional life. Why had she been willing to settle in her personal one? Luke hadn't deserved her. She should have sent him packing long before she had. Being alone was better than being with someone who made himself feel better by belittling you.

"Laughing and dancing until the end sounds like a good plan for everyone to have," she agreed. "Few seem to achieve it, though."

Despite having gone through a few rough patches, her parents loved each other, but they weren't laughing and dancing kind of people. Maybe because of her mother's traumatic birth and having been raised by a grieving father. Ivy couldn't say she'd been a laughing, dancing kind of person with Luke, either. She'd enjoyed the good parts of their relationship, especially in the early days, but she'd never looked at him the way her grandmother had looked at Gramps. Nor had he ever looked at her the way Gramps had Grammie.

"We aren't laughing and dancing at this moment of our relatively young lives." Eyes twinkling, Caleb nudged her with his elbow. "We need to do something about that. Dance with me?"

Excitement bubbling through her, Ivy eyed him. "Did you set me up to feel as if I couldn't say no to dancing with you without contradicting what I just agreed to?"

His grin was lethal. "Whatever makes you think that I'd do something like that? I'm just trying to make sure you're laughing and dancing and enjoying your present."

Oh, yeah, he'd set that one up perfectly. The way her heart raced said she didn't mind one bit, either. Ugh. What was wrong with her? She knew better than to get caught up with Caleb. As wonderful as he was in this controlled environment, eventually he'd be no different than Luke or the others back home.

Standing, he held out his hand. "Come on, Doc. Let's dance."

Why did taking his hand seem like such a big deal? As if, if she put her hand in his she'd never be quite the same? It wasn't as if she hadn't held his hand yesterday. But this felt more meaningful. More revealing.

She gulped back her own imaginings, because that was all this was. She wasn't the prettiest flower, and he wasn't picking her. He just wanted to dance and enjoy life.

"Just remember you asked for this, because I never said I could dance." She placed her hand in his, marveling at the instant electricity of the skin-to-skin contact.

"The same could be said about me."

"If not, asking me to dance doesn't seem a wise decision."

His eyes twinkled. "Let's just say that I wanted to dance with the most beautiful woman here enough to risk exposing my dancing skills, whatever they may be. Especially since she'd been eyeing the dance floor with longing to join the others."

Had she? Maybe. Everyone seemed to be having so much fun. She had a good life and had enjoyed time with her fellow residents, but how long had it been since she'd done something just for the fun of it? Since before her breakup with Luke, before Gramps had died, since… It had been much too long. She'd not gone in to this trip thinking it would be fun, but it was, a lot of which she attributed to the man holding her hand as he led her toward the dance floor.

Holding Caleb's hand for the second day in a row was so not why she felt giddy. Or, maybe, it was.

"You may regret this. I wasn't kidding about not being much of a dancer. I mean, I know the moves to several dances, but can never relax enough to be any good." She gave a nervous laugh. "Does that make sense?"

"Tonight's about having fun, Doc, not perfection. Don't sweat whether or not you know the steps. Just move however, and wherever, the music leads you."

"What if it leads me off a cliff?" she teased, marveling at him.

"Then we'll hope there's water beneath so we can go for a swim." He began to move in a similar fashion to the other dancers to the upbeat song. "Don't let what anyone else thinks keep you from enjoying yourself." His eyes sparkled as he pulled her to him and leaned near her ear. "How likely is it that you will ever see any of these people again?"

"Well, that's just sad." She felt so close to the veterans and their families, not to mention the crew and wonderful French people they'd met. And then there was Caleb. She'd been with him almost nonstop. She would see Caleb again. He'd said he made calls to the hospital. Thank goodness as the thought of not seeing him again put her stomach in a vise.

"But realistic, unfortunately." He gave her hand a gentle squeeze and slowly turned her on the dance floor. "Do you think you'll come back next year?"

"Maybe." She could smell his spicy scent and fought leaning just a little closer to brush her cheek against his to feel the very slight stubble she'd find there. "They may not ask me."

He pulled back, arching his brow. "After the incident on the plane and how you handled it so smoothly, they'll ask. You're a shoo-in for life."

"Right place at the right time with the right medicines," she said, her senses full of how close he was. How his palm rested on her low back and his other was pressed against hers. How if she took a step forward her body would similarly be pressed against his. The song wasn't slow but wasn't fast, either, to where there was a huge variety of movements happening on the dance floor. It would be easy to close that distance, lean against Caleb and forget anyone else was even there.

"It was more than that, but it's too gorgeous of a night to argue over the specifics. You rocked the plane. You've rocked this trip." Eyes twinkling, he lifted their hands in an exaggerated movement, swaying his hips to the side as he did so, then grinning when she laughed. "I'm glad I get to be a small part of your greatness."

His compliment spread heat through her. Luke

would never have acknowledged her role in what had happened on the plane and that Caleb appreciated her efforts made her feel good, and a little embarrassed. Then again, Luke hadn't been all negative. In the beginning, he'd been nice, complimentary and somewhat supportive.

"I could say the same about you." She attempted to ground herself with recalling that all attractions were exciting in the beginning. Whatever was between her and Caleb was new and that's why it felt so good, so right.

From the dance floor, Delphine spotted them. The French woman waved, then laughed as her husband spun her around, dipping her back.

"Yeah, I don't do that." Ivy suspected that Caleb was a much better dancer than the simple moves they were doing. His body held a grace that said he could move any way he liked and with finesse. His dance moves were fluid, graceful, tantalizing, even. Would his lovemaking be the same? Not rushed or selfish, but a pleasurable dance of his body meshing with hers? Gulping back at the heat seizing her, Ivy squeezed her eyes closed, trying to clear her mind. She didn't need to be thinking of Caleb that way. Only, closing her eyes made her more aware of his hands touching her, of his spicy scent, of the energy of his body near hers.

"No need to close your eyes, Doc. I won't dip

you back if you don't want dipped," he promised, chuckling. "However, for the record, I'd never let you fall."

Please be telling the truth. Please don't let me fall for you.

Knowing that wasn't what he'd meant but desperately wishing it was, Ivy opened her eyes, replacing her mental image of Caleb with an up close one of him staring into her eyes. Although his tone had been light and he'd had that husky chuckle, there was a seriousness in those amber eyes that made breathing difficult.

"There's no worry that you might cause me to fall so long as you don't dip me back."

Oh, Caleb. What's happening here?

"How about we just go with the music and have fun?"

It's what she needed to do rather than overanalyzing the moment.

"Is that not what we're doing?" His gaze searched hers. "Dancing and laughing until our dying day, remember?"

The light in his eyes hinted that he'd read her thoughts. Read them, knew she'd been thinking of things much more serious than dancing. Although that light twinkled brightly, it didn't hide that she wasn't the only one concerned over what could happen between them if they let it.

"Quit."

She swallowed. "What?"

"Thinking about whatever caused that look on your face."

"I was thinking about you." So much for not telling him her thoughts. No matter. He knew. He knew so much more than what she wished he knew, and yet, he didn't really know her, did he? They were in a romantic bubble in France that would burst the moment they returned to reality. Men like him would eventually resent her success, would eventually feel the need to pull her down. Luke had taught her that lesson well. She didn't need a repeat course.

"Thinking of me made you grimace? I'm going to have to do something about that. Or at least earn the reaction." With that, he playfully spun her as Phillipe had done with Delphine. Ivy kept up with the beat he set as best she could, grateful for the distraction, laughing and shaking off her missteps.

"Much better," he assured. "This is how I want to see your face. Smiling with joy." With a mischievousness in his eyes, he dipped her back, keeping her secure within his hands as the song came to an end.

"Caleb!" she screeched, clasping onto his arm. Not that it was necessary. The movement was fast, sure, and at no point did he not have a secure hold.

When she rose, he pulled her to him, her body close, and looked directly into her eyes. What she saw there stole her breath much more so than the dip had. She was imagining things. Had to be. In her happy fairy-tale bubble, he was looking at her like Gramps had looked at Grammie when they'd been dancing around the kitchen. Obviously, Ivy was hallucinating, just seeing what she wanted to see.

"See." Did he sound a little breathless, too? "I told you I wouldn't let you fall."

"What happened to you saying you wouldn't dip me if I didn't want dipped?"

He pretended confusion. "Did you say that you didn't want me to dip you back? Or just that if I didn't, then I wouldn't have to worry about letting you fall?" His gaze held hers. "I was never worried that you'd fall, Doc. Trust me."

Trust him? What if it was herself that she didn't trust? What if her track record was so bad that she'd already struck out of the relationship game? What if every cell in her body wanted to clamor closer and that terrified her? Even if she wanted to trust him, she doubted she'd ever trust any man again. Luke and the others had permanently ruined that for her. Caleb was wonderful, but this wasn't real life. She needed to remember that.

They danced the slow dance, Ivy painfully cognizant of everything about him. When the music changed to a faster number, they continued to dance. Caleb seemed determined that she have a good time. Appreciating his efforts, she did her best to do just that. It was so easy to have fun with Caleb, but the physical tension she felt when near him never let go. Her awareness of him, his broad shoulders that her hands rested upon, the strong lines of his nape where her fingers brushed over his hair, the thick strength of his chest and the narrowness of his waist, the warmness of his smile and eyes as they looked into hers, had her insides winding tighter and tighter. She'd never been one to be overcome with physical desire, but Caleb made her want to forego logic and just feel everything that he elicited within her body.

She wouldn't. To do that would be much too complicated. But that didn't mean she was oblivious to how sexually aware he made her feel. The way he looked at her, touched her arms, her waist, held her hands…he made her feel desirable, as if she was the most beautiful woman in the room and he only had eyes for her.

Like the prettiest flower in the garden and he'd picked her.

Caleb didn't feel that way about her, so the comparison was ridiculous. Still, as another slow song came on and they moved together, his heartbeat beneath her cheek where it was pressed against his chest, lulled her so that, temporarily, it was okay to just pretend.

For the moment, resting against a man like

Caleb was quite nice because she knew he really was strong enough to catch her, not that he'd have to because his hands were secure at her waist, warming her low back as their bodies swayed to the beat. It was probably her imagination, but she'd swear his lips brushed her hair, pressing a soft kiss there. If he had, he didn't comment and neither did she because the sensation was so brief, so light, she truly couldn't decide if it had really happened.

Delphine and Phillipe were chatty during the drive back to their home. Caleb chatted back. Ivy made noises every so often and was proud she managed that with Caleb's hand clasping hers in the car's dimly lit back seat.

When they got back to the house, Phillipe asked Caleb to help him with moving something. Ivy went on upstairs, got ready for bed, listened for him to come up the stairs. When he did, she yanked the door open, but filled with disappointment that he'd gone into his room and closed the door.

She stood there a moment, wondering what she was doing, what she'd have done had he been in the hallway.

Not anything good.

The veterans had the morning off to rest prior to the following day when they'd have a big ceremony in Colleville recognizing the date. Ivy smiled at Caleb when she came downstairs, not surprised to find him already there. He sat at the table with Phillipe, Fred and Trista, drinking coffee and eating slices of Delphine's delicious bread.

"Good morning, Ivy. I was just asking Caleb if you had been to the church at Angoville yet." Trista took a sip from her coffee bowl. "It's one of my favorite places to visit. With your medical backgrounds, I imagine you two will feel the same."

"We'd love to visit the church."

"Take my car. I will be working here this morning," Phillipe told them.

Ivy had first heard of the church, which had been set up as a medical station to treat the wounded, from her grandfather. Two American medics had worked through the night, caring for all wounded regardless of which side they fought for. It had been one of Gramps's favorite stories to tell.

Within the hour they were at the church, with its weathered tombstones marking family gravesites. No one else was at the out-of-the-ordinary tourist stop site.

"One of the medics requested to be buried here. His ashes were brought here at a later time. There's a marker in his honor to the front of the church," she told Caleb, opening the heavy wooden side door and entering the church. As with many of the places they'd visited, evidence of the past had left its mark on the building and its contents.

"The medics used the pews as beds for the wounded. The stains are from that night. They saved a lot of lives." Ivy ran her hand over a pew's worn smooth armrest. A wounded soldier had bled there. Had he been saved? "During the bombings, the church windows were shattered," she continued, moving away to stare up at one of the windows. "The French replaced some with stained glass honoring the paratroopers. Those are the two medics." She pointed to the names beneath an image of the Statue of Liberty.

"It blows my mind at how they honored the paratroopers." Caleb stared up at the stained glass.

"I wish Gramps could have seen this, everything we're seeing during this trip, so he'd know what a difference he and his fellow soldiers made."

This trip had meant so much to him. He should have been there. Should have been at her side, teasing her and showing her places he'd seen, things he'd done, finding the healing these trips were meant to bring. Ivy turned, her gaze going back to a pew stain. Emotion flooded through her. Grief, sadness, anger that he was gone and maybe even fear over how entangled she'd become with Caleb. No wonder, with how her heart had been so raw from missing Gramps. Sitting, she stared toward the altar and let her tears flow. "Why did he have to die? He should have been here with me."

Her question was a rhetorical one, so she was surprised when Caleb sat down next to her and answered.

"Everyone dies, Ivy. Everyone."

"I know that. It's just…" She swiped at her eyes. "I miss him. I had to finish residency and then there was this trip, and I've held it together, but I ache that he isn't here, that he's never going to be here again."

Caleb wrapped his arm around her and pulled her close, letting her bury her face against the strength of his shoulder. "I'm truly sorry for your loss, Ivy."

Leaning against him, Ivy quit fighting her tears and let the sobs rack her body. "He was almost a hundred, but he was vibrant, Caleb. I wasn't expecting him to die. Maybe I should have been, but I wasn't. Not yet."

"You loved him."

She nodded. "More than anything or anyone. He was my hero."

"How wonderful to have someone like that in your life to look up to."

Sniffling, she raised up to look at him. "You're right. I know you're right, but it doesn't make the pain any less. Sorry I let loose with the tears that way."

"Don't be sorry for grieving your grandfather."

"It's more that I cried in front of you. I don't want you to think I'm weak."

He snorted softly. "No worries there. I'd pit your strength and determination against anyone's."

"Really?"

Wiping his thumb across her wet cheek, he nodded. "You're an amazingly strong person, Ivy. I imagine you get that trait from your grandfather. Because of that and many other reasons, he'll never really be far away, because he'll live on through you."

Ivy blinked at him in awe. "Were you also a psychologist in the service?"

"The forced recipient of one's services a few times."

Flinching at the things he must have seen and done, Ivy stared into his eyes. Last night she'd been so caught up in the physical. This morning the attraction was still there, but it was something more she felt as she looked into his beautiful eyes. Something that spread through her, threatening to consume her, and leaving her both afraid and grateful to have met him. "Well, you must have learned a few things. I've kept all that bottled up inside me since Gramps's death. I think part of me has been in denial right up until the night before we left to come here and my grief has been waiting to burst free ever since we arrived."

"It's okay to grieve, Ivy, to cry for the loss of someone you love. That's straight from me, not the psychiatrist. Although they probably all said the same to me several times."

He'd been through so much, seen so much, and yet was full of strength and goodness. "Do you ever cry, Caleb?" she wondered out loud.

His gaze shifted to the paratrooper on the stained glass window. "Not in a long time."

He took her hand into his, lifted it to his lips and pressed a kiss there. "This church is still a place of healing, isn't it?"

"It must be." She took a deep breath. "I feel more at peace than I've felt in months."

Maybe the two paratroopers' spirits lived on, healing those who ventured inside their church's walls. Or maybe it was the man sitting beside her.

CHAPTER NINE

AFTER IVY AND CALEB returned to Phillipe and Delphine's, Ivy went through the motions, was fairly certain she said the right things at the right times as no one called her out for verbal bumblings, but she couldn't stop thinking about Caleb. Sweet, wonderful Caleb who had held her while she cried, and made it easy to lean on him, to be comforted by him, to not feel as if she had to keep up her defenses even when she knew she should.

Hadn't she promised herself that she was not going to become involved? Caleb hadn't done anything to make her think he was like her exes. Quite the opposite, and that scared her more than anything Luke and the others ever had the power to do.

Caleb was different.

Late that night, she sat on her bed, toying with a frayed quilt edge while waiting for Caleb to finish in their shared bathroom. He'd offered to let her get ready for bed first, but she'd insisted he go ahead. As tired as she was, her mind raced with trying to figure out things she wasn't going to solve in a single night. She flopped back on the time-softened quilt and stared up at the old wooden beam supports that made up the room's ceiling.

How could she sleep when her mind was filled with what-ifs, maybes and reminders of all the reasons why she shouldn't be interested in Caleb beyond friendship. None of which convinced her body that Caleb as anything more than a friend was off-limits. This wasn't some have-a-quick-fling getaway. She didn't have flings. She didn't. Never had. Never would.

So why did her pulse kick up at the thought of marching into the bathroom, taking his tooth-brush out of his hand and tasting the minty flavor on his breath as she kissed him so thoroughly that it left him breathless?

Kissing Caleb would be a mistake. Pleasurable, but still a mistake.

A rustling sounded in the hallway, then there was a light knock on her door. Ivy held her breath as if he was somehow going to hear the air moving in and out of her lungs. She worried she wasn't strong enough to see him and not give in to throwing her arms around him and kissing him until the world, and logic, subsided.

"I'm finished," he called through the solid wood. "The bathroom is yours."

Thinking it better if he thought she'd gone to sleep rather than her seeing him again when her tired mind was playing with her common sense, Ivy waited more than half an hour after she'd heard his bedroom door close prior to getting off her bed.

Still thinking on Caleb and how she needed to keep reality in focus, she quietly gathered her toiletries and pajamas. Being in France, in Normandy where she'd planned to go with Gramps, she was projecting things onto Caleb that just wouldn't hold the test of time. Admitting that to herself was vital. Everything felt magical and more intense because of where they were, because of her emotional state prior to even meeting Caleb. Once they were back to their ordinary lives, the sparks between them wouldn't feel so electric or shine so brightly.

What if it didn't end, though? What if Caleb wouldn't be threatened by her independence? By the fact that she made more money than him? What if he'd never feel the need to insult her intelligence or tear down her confidence?

Who was she kidding? Caleb was a gorgeous alpha male. She was an average female with a terrible track record with men. Of course, they'd end. To think otherwise would be nothing short of foolishness.

She opened the bedroom door. A barefoot Caleb wearing a T-shirt and loose shorts stood in the hallway. He looked almost as startled as she was. "Caleb!"

That her opening the door had caught him off guard said a lot regarding his state of mind as she doubted much took the former paratrooper by surprise. Why was he outside her door? She'd heard him go into his room, but not when he'd returned. She was obviously a mess.

Why did he come back?

Why talking to Ivy felt so imperative that Caleb had gotten out of bed made no sense. Which was why he'd hesitated outside her door for longer than he cared to admit. He would see her the following day and night as they went through the D-Day ceremonies, and the following day they'd tour the Collins Museum, then head to Paris overnight prior to catching their flight. They'd have plenty of time to talk. Yet, he hadn't been able to stay in bed. Not when he'd known she'd been awake and was ignoring his knock rather than face him. Had she thought he'd knocked on her door with hopes of an invite into her room? That hadn't been his intent. But if it had, why would she pretend to be asleep? He'd swear she was interested in him, too. Him the person and not his parents' bank account the way Katrina had mainly been. Ivy didn't even know about his parents' shipping business.

"You don't have to pretend to be asleep or

avoid me, Ivy," he assured. "Surely, you know that I'd never pressure you for something you didn't want."

Not that he didn't want her. He did. He wanted to kiss her. To lift her loosened hair and press his lips to the curve of her neck and work his way around to nuzzle her ear where he would whisper all the things he wanted to do to her, with her. He wanted—

"I thought it best if we didn't see each other again tonight."

"Because?"

"I don't want to do something I'll regret."

"You're positive you'd regret something happening between us?"

"I—I'm not sure. The past two weeks have been wonderful, but they're not the real world." Her tone doused him with cold rejection. "I've just finished residency and have a lot of life changes. I'm starting a new job, moving to my grandfather's farm, and then, there's the whole breakup with Luke. He cheated on me, had been cheating for months, and he's not the first man in my life to do so."

"I'm not a cheater, Ivy. If we were in a relationship, I'd be faithful and expect the same from you." Was that what he wanted? To be in a relationship with Ivy? Was that why he'd come to her door?

"I-it's not that I don't believe you, it's just that

the past few months have been so full of changes that I need to find balance and peace in my life." Her gaze connected with his, and were big, blue and full of doubt. "Spending time with you once we're back in Knoxville doesn't feel conducive to those things."

Katrina's barbs echoed through his mind, her accusations that he wasn't good enough, wasn't worth her time if he didn't come attached to his parents' bank account. Broken. That's what she'd called him. Mentally, emotionally and physically broken. Did Ivy see him in the same light? He hadn't thought so, but maybe she was right. Maybe the attraction between them only existed because of their enforced confinement.

"Going to dinner with a friend isn't conducive to your finding balance and peace?" He kept his voice neutral as best as he could considering his level of frustration.

Ivy's tongue darted out, moistening the corner of her mouth. Had he moved closer or had she? He could feel her body heat, could feel the magnetic pull of her body to his.

"Is that why you're outside my bedroom door, Caleb? To ask me to go to dinner with you as a friend once we're back in Knoxville? Because I'm not buying that." Her gaze dropped to his lips. "You kissed me in Carentan. On the dance floor, I felt your lips against my hair. I wasn't sure at first, but you did, didn't you?"

"I did." Just a gentle touching of his lips before he'd caught himself and pulled back. He'd had no right to kiss her and certainly shouldn't have in such a public place. All the quick kiss had done was leave him hungry for more.

"That kiss didn't feel friendly." Her hands went to his chest, perhaps to put a barrier between them as their bodies were almost touching, but the movement had the opposite effect. Her warm fingers burned through the thin cotton of his T-shirt.

"No? Then I did it all wrong."

She stared at him in confusion. "What do you mean? Wrong?"

What did he mean? Great question. He wasn't sure he knew. What he did know was that he wanted Ivy more than he'd wanted anything in a long time. He understood her concerns. He had ones of his own, but that didn't stop him from wanting her.

"I've never been that great with words, Doc. I'm more a man of action."

"I—" Her throat worked. The blue of her eyes darkened in the hallway's shadows. Her pulse throbbed at her throat. Her chin lifted. Challenge, and something more, shone on her face. "Okay, then no words. Show me."

Caleb's heart pounded at the brevity of what she was saying. He lost himself in her gaze long enough to be sure he'd not misinterpreted, then captured her lower lip between his, and eyes locked with hers, he gave a slow, gentle tug on the plump flesh.

"That doesn't feel friendly, either," she whispered against his mouth, her voice hoarse. Her hands splayed against his pecs, but rather than push him away, they slid over his chest, settling on his shoulders.

"No? I'll have to do better." With that he gave in to the hunger burning inside him and kissed Ivy. He kissed her so thoroughly, so hungrily, so completely that he struggled to know where he ended and she began. Her fingers were at his nape, pulling him closer as she kissed him back. Never had he experienced anything like kissing Ivy McEwen. Never. The closest thing he could liken the giddy sensations assailing him was to those first moments of jumping prior to opening his chute when he was free-falling. Until her, nothing had compared to the rush, to the peace of shutting out the whole world to focus on the moment, to the inherent danger that came with what he was doing.

Kissing Ivy was free-falling.

He was falling.

For Ivy.

They kissed for what felt a lifetime and yet ended much too soon. When their lips parted, he saw the invitation in her eyes. All he had to do was march her two steps back into her room, close the door, and he could spend the night exploring every tantalizing inch of her. He was tempted to do just that, to make love to her so thoroughly that she couldn't deny what was happening between them.

But lurking hesitation also darkened her eyes. It was that hesitation, knowing she'd regret anything they did come morning, that gave him the willpower to step back rather than into her room. Even if he never got another chance to make love to Ivy, he couldn't in good conscience do so tonight when he knew she wasn't fully on board. She wanted to, but she'd blame it on the late hour and being caught up in the moment. If they made love, he didn't want her looking for excuses on why it had happened.

He cupped her face, stared down into her beautiful face. Unable to resist one last taste, he kissed her again then pulled away before he reached the point to where he lost the will to do so.

"I'm going to go to my room now, Ivy, but not because I don't want to carry you into your room."

Her eyes widened, obviously surprised. "I, um, okay. If that's what you want."

Caleb wanted a lot of things, but for tonight, her answer was all that he'd get. When he did make love to Ivy, she'd have no regrets. Not regrets like the ones his body already had that he'd be spending the night alone in his room down the hallway rather than with the woman who was backing away from him physically and emotionally, because uncertainty now far outweighed the eagerness he'd witnessed only moments before. What was it about her that made him want her to trust him enough to come to him with no hesitations, and for him to be enough just as he was?

If not spending the night alone had been his end game, then he'd have never walked away. Which begged the question: What was his end game where Ivy was concerned? Did he have one, or was she right that they were just caught up in their close proximity?

Their midmorning Collins Museum tour was their last scheduled event of the trip. The Château de Franquetot had been purchased several years prior with the new owners turning the rundown castle into a museum. Now the home was much as it had been when used as the army headquarters. The owner himself greeted them, giving their veterans a private tour, and even allowing Owen to sit in a chair at a desk General Eisenhower had once used. Although she still battled with the sting of his rejection, Ivy laughed when Caleb picked out more key chains from the gift shop.

He scooped up a few more. "What?"

"I'm wondering if you truly have that many

friends or if you've got a problem and secretly hoard key chains."

"You've figured me out." His grin had her heart flopping around as if it had forgotten how to properly beat.

"Not even close," she said before she could think better of it.

He didn't seem fazed, just continued smiling as he put the key chains on the counter, then paid for them. Ordering her pulse to calm down, Ivy thumbed through some postcards. She paused at one that was of the church in Angoville-au-Plain.

"You should get that one."

Recalling how she'd sobbed into his shoulder there, Ivy frowned and put the card back. "You forget my aversion to touristy trinkets."

"Here." He removed the card she'd just re-placed. "I'm buying this for you."

Heat flooded through her body. "I don't need a postcard, Caleb."

"Sure, you do. If nothing else, you can add it to your trunk."

"That trunk is at my parents' house." She watched as he selected a few more postcards. "What are you doing?"

"Buying postcards. You should pick something to give to your parents. You mentioned doing so to be funny."

"I'm not that funny."

"You make me smile."

Ivy's cheeks heated further. Yeah, she imagined she had. He'd probably been laughing his butt off at her expense two nights ago. The day before he'd acted as if nothing had happened, smiling frequently, but she'd felt awkward. Fortunately, with it being June 6, their schedule had been packed, starting with the ceremony in Colleville at the American Cemetery and ending with a farewell dinner hosted by a local veterans' organization. Not once had he acted as if anything unusual had happened the night before and by the time Ivy had gone to bed, she'd almost questioned if she'd dreamed his kiss and what followed.

"My parents haven't visited Normandy but have been to Paris several times. That's much more their style of traveling." As they'd loved history, she might have questioned that except her mother had an aversion to most things that had to do with Gramps.

"It's not on a lot of folks' top vacation spots."

"If they'd ever been here, seen the way it is now, it would be." It truly was one of the most gorgeous places she'd ever been. "The wide-open green fields, the gorgeous coastline and beaches, and the people who are so wonderful."

"We'll have to come back."

Her gaze cut to his, but he'd turned toward the cashier and was paying for the postcard.

She studied his profile, wondering why her

heart flew at such an innocent comment. He hadn't meant they come back as in they come back *together* but rather as part of SMVF. Of course, that was what he'd meant. It was all she'd wanted him to mean. Anything more would just complicate an already complicated situation.

Frustrated with herself, she left the gift shop and headed toward the small restaurant at the other end of the main floor. Groups of soldiers and reenactors laughed and shared stories. It was a merry scene and somehow grated on Ivy, to where she opted to wait outdoors instead of inside with the others.

Mary followed her. "I can't believe it's over and that we're about to head back to Paris."

Ivy couldn't, either. This time the following day they'd be on their flight home. Then what? Other than the panic attacks she was sure to have while on the plane, that is.

"Hopefully, we'll make it there in time to see some of the sites," Mary continued, sounding wistful. "I've never seen the Eiffel Tower."

"This was my first time to Europe, so I've never seen it, either," Ivy admitted. "Once we get settled into the hotel, we'll hire a car. We can't be in Paris and not see the Eiffel Tower."

Several of the others wanted to go, too, as most hadn't seen the iconic tower. Slade and Suzie were quite enthusiastic about going, just as they'd become quite enthusiastic about each other. They didn't mind who knew as they held hands and looked at each other with googly eyes. Oh, to be so young and naive that it always started that way but ended with one party's heart broken. In Ivy's case, it was always her.

Mary nudged her. "You look at Caleb the same way as those two lovebirds."

"Stop it," she told Mary, shaking her head. "You're mistaken."

Mary obviously didn't believe her as she grinned and asked, "Are you going to see him when we get back to Knoxville?"

"I imagine we'll see each other at the hospital from time to time." Would it be torture to see him, or a reminder of a close call she'd narrowly escaped?

Mary's gaze met Ivy's. "Not what I meant, but also not my business. Sorry."

Ivy sighed. "It's okay. I just don't know how else to answer. Caleb is a great guy, but we're just friends." Were they even that? Recalling his "friendly" kiss, Ivy swallowed. What had his kisses meant? His walking away? How could he act so normal, as if nothing had happened, when she wanted to demand answers from him? Had he lain in bed the night before thinking about their hallway encounter? Had he closed his eyes and relived the feel of his lips against hers the way that she'd done? Probably not. Otherwise, how could he be so casually relaxed around her when she was wound tighter than the Gordian knot.

Mary gave her a disappointed look, then her eyes brightened. "There's still time. We should invite Caleb to go with us tonight."

"Go with you where?" Caleb joined where they stood on the lawn. Had Mary seen him walking toward them and that's why she'd said what she'd said, knowing he'd hear? Not that Ivy wouldn't have invited him to go. Anyone from their group was welcome. Caleb had done nothing wrong other than witness her embarrassing surrender to their chemistry. Thank goodness he'd not done the same or their last two days would have been tough.

"To the Eiffel Tower," Mary supplied before Ivy could. "We're hoping to arrive in Paris in time to see the tower for ourselves."

Caleb turned toward Ivy. "You realize the Eiffel Tower is about an hour's drive from the airport hotel where we'll be staying?"

Ivy winced. No, she hadn't realized. She should have looked at a map. Paris was a big city. Disappointment showed on Mary's face and Ivy made a quick decision. "How far away it is doesn't matter. We're going to the Eiffel Tower even if it means we don't sleep until we're on the plane. We can't come all this way and not see France's most iconic structure." When else was she going to be in Paris? Probably never. "Getting our veterans on and off the train wouldn't be easy, so we'll splurge and hire a driver. More than one, if needed. We'll figure it out after we get to the hotel and know our time frame and who wants to go."

Mary clasped her hands together. "This is exciting. I've always dreamed of seeing the Eiffel Tower. I'm so glad we're going for it."

Not looking directly toward Caleb, Ivy nodded. "Sometimes life only gives us one opportunity to do certain things. If we choose to let them pass us by, we'll regret it forever."

Caleb's brow lifted. She hadn't consciously aimed the comment at him, but if the shoe fit… unfortunately, she suspected that she was going to be the one living with regrets.

CHAPTER TEN

By THE TIME they'd ridden the four hours from Normandy to the airport, the veterans were too tired to want to travel into central Paris. Doing so would put them arriving back at the hotel after midnight. Knowing it was his last night in France with Ivy, Caleb could push through any fatigue. At some point before they arrived back in Knoxville, they needed to talk. He'd upset her with leaving her room and he wanted to set the record straight to make sure she understood why he'd done what he had. They'd had their busiest schedule the day prior and hadn't had a chance to talk. At some point prior to arriving in Knoxville, he'd make sure they found time.

"We can't leave the veterans here without medical." Disappointment shone on Ivy's face. "I'll make arrangements for cars to pick up those going, and I'll stay to keep watch on those staying here."

"I'll stay," Caleb offered. He couldn't imagine anyone he'd rather see the Eiffel Tower with than

Ivy, but if they couldn't both leave the hotel, he wasn't going at the expense of Ivy being able to.

"No, I will," she immediately countered, not surprising Caleb. To the end, she viewed taking care of the veterans as mainly her responsibility and she put that first.

He started to insist he be the one to stay, but Lara shook her head. "Both of you go. I was on the fence anyway. I'm worn out and saw the tower when my husband and I visited Paris last fall." When Ivy started to protest, the nurse shook her head. "No, really, go. I'm looking forward to changing into something comfy and relaxing." When Ivy started to protest more, Lara gave her a pointed look. "Go. I'll make sure all the guys are safely in their rooms and be here if they need anything. Y'all have taken care of most everything on this trip. Let me do this. Have fun and take lots of photos."

Caleb shot the nurse a grateful smile. He owed her big for the extra time with Ivy, especially with it being a whirlwind night viewing of Paris's most iconic tourist spot. "Thanks, Lara."

Once at the hotel, a local helped arrange for a hired van to drive them for short stops at a couple of central Paris sites with a longer stop planned at the tower. Seven of their group ended up in the van. The thirtyish-years-old French driver took them to the Arc de Triomphe first. The talkative man pulled the van to the side of the road.

Laughing, they jumped out, snapped photos, including a group shot taken by their driver, then hopped back into the van. Their next stop was the Louvre. Slade and Suzie were all giggly as they posed for pictures with their fingers touching the top of the glass pyramid. Everyone took similar staged photos, making silly poses, then marveling at the architecture.

"How gorgeous this must be in the daylight where you can make out the intricate details," Ivy mused, staring in awe at the museum.

"It's amazing," Caleb agreed, enthralled with her expression as much as he was with the magnificent building. "Just as you are. Thanks for making this happen. The others are having a great time."

Her gaze cut to his, challenge sparkling there that he knew was rooted in his having gone back to his room. "But you're not?"

"I thought that was a given." But maybe not. They needed to talk. In private.

Ivy eyed him a moment, then went back to taking in the museum. "I'd love to come back and just wander around. I bet you could spend an entire day and not get close to seeing everything."

"Probably not. The *Mona Lisa* is here," he said. "If we saw her, do you think we could figure out what she was smiling at?"

Ivy's brow lifted. "Opposed to the millions of others who've seen her and speculated?"

Caleb laughed. "I have my theories."

"Okay, now you have me curious. What are your theories on why da Vinci painted her smiling?"

"It's obvious." Pausing for effect, he kept a straight face. "To make us wonder."

Ivy rolled her eyes. "Brilliant. The mystery is solved."

He chuckled. "Seriously, it's the smile that gets folks to talking. Who was there with them? Or was anyone? Who was she thinking about? A lover, perhaps?"

"Of course, you'd wonder that."

His gaze cut to hers. "Why 'of course'?"

"Because you're a man." Even as she said it, she averted her eyes and he'd swear she was blushing.

Knowing she was thinking about the other night and not wanting her to throw additional walls up, he puffed out his chest. "Glad you've noticed."

"Difficult not to."

"Good. I want you to notice."

Her gaze narrowed. "Really? Because that's not the impression you gave the other night."

He held up his hand. "We need to talk, but now's not the time. Mary's on her way over here. So, we'll just enjoy Paris with our friends and each other. Deal?"

Looking torn, she sighed. "You're right. It's

our last night in France. Who wants to dwell on past mistakes?"

He'd like to question her on just what past mistakes she meant, but Mary was walking toward them. He had a pretty good idea, anyway. He hadn't been wrong to go to his room, but he had dwelt on doing so. Mostly because he kept questioning why he had felt he needed to. Why hadn't he just taken what Ivy offered? Why had it mattered so much to him that she freely give herself to him rather than just be caught up in a passionate moment?

Wouldn't that only make sense if he wanted something more from Ivy than just a night or two? He'd not wanted that since Katrina. Since the first round of their relationship, because he realized he'd never wanted more from Katrina the second time, when he'd been laid up in a hospital bed, mourning his best friend's death and the loss of his career. She'd swooped in, beautiful and breaking up the boredom of his hospital stay, and he'd let her because he had nothing else to do beyond rehabilitating his busted body. When she'd given him the ultimatum of "making something of his life" or losing her, saying goodbye was easy. Much easier than saying goodbye to Ivy would be after only knowing her two weeks.

"Come on, guys. Our driver is ready to roll," Mary called, gesturing to the parked van.

They got back in, oohing and ahhing as they

crossed the Pont de Bir-Hakeim. The Frenchman drove them the short distance to the Eiffel Tower, then pulled over for them to jump out, telling them he'd arrive in an hour to the exact spot so they could return to their hotel.

Street vendors were along the sidewalk leading to the tower. They sold everything from balloons to sparkling replicas of the majestic structure towering above them.

"I read that the tower twinkles like a Christmas tree for five minutes on the hour each night," Mary enthused. "Look at how magnificent it is lit. I think seeing the tower at night is better than if we'd come during the daylight."

"That's awesome that we'll get to witness the twinkling lights," Ivy agreed as they continued to walk toward the tower's base. "It's surreal that we're in Paris, looking up at the Eiffel Tower. It really is magnificent."

"Let's take photos here," Linda suggested. "If we get too close it'll be more difficult to get all of the tower in the shot."

"Good point."

They paused and took group shots with Caleb holding his cell phone as far out in front of him as his arm would reach. He angled his hand to where he could get as much of their entourage and the tower as possible.

Slade and Suzie took multiple selfies, then had Linda take a picture of them. When done, they took off, saying they were going to watch the tower from the bridge.

"Here, let me take a picture of you and Ivy with the tower in the background." Mary reached for his phone and Caleb handed it over.

Ivy's eyes narrowed for the briefest second, but she smiled as Mary took several photos.

Mary handed back his phone, then looked ahead as a couple vacated a bench where they'd been sitting. "I'm going to snag that bench and watch the lights from there."

"Me, too," Linda said, joining her, and patting the bench. "Jimmy," she said to the son of one of the veterans. "There's room if you want to keep two ladies company."

Everyone other than Ivy and Caleb opted to view the tower without walking to the park.

She turned to him as soon as they were outside hearing range. "Did you pay them to do that?"

He feigned innocence. "To do what?"

"Ditch us for a bench so we'd be alone." She eyed him suspiciously.

"Not me, but I wouldn't put it past Mary." He glanced toward her, making eye contact. "I can't say I'm sorry, though."

"That we got ditched?"

He nodded. "I like them, but I'd rather see the Eiffel Tower with you without an audience."

She didn't say anything in response to his comment, just looked away to stare up at the tower.

"It's such an iconic place that I've seen photos of so many times that actually being here doesn't feel real."

Being at the Eiffel Tower with Ivy, strolling toward the base, just the two of them, was surreal. The moon was bright above them, casting an almost magical blue hue to the night sky. With the tower magnificently jutting upward, they could be walking into a movie scene. A romantic one. One where he got to be the hero, without flaws or a past.

He reached for Ivy's hand and was grateful she didn't pull away. Maybe she was caught up in the magic of where they were, too, because she clasped his hand, giving it a slight squeeze.

"This trip was everything it should have been, except that Gramps wasn't here."

His heart ached at how much grief he heard in her voice for her grandfather. Holding her while she'd cried at the Angoville church had about gutted him. He understood grief. Not a day went by that he didn't miss Blake. "He'd be so proud of you, Ivy."

Just as Blake would be proud of him for what he'd accomplished in Knoxville, for being there to help his wife, Jordan make the ambulance service a success.

Pausing, Ivy turned toward him, her big blue eyes pinning him with the yearning in them. "How can you know that?"

Brushing a hair back from her face, he nodded. "Because any grandfather or parent would be proud to be related to you."

Swallowing, she gave a nervous laugh. "Maybe. I'm not always easy to live with."

"I'll make a note of it."

Her eyes widened.

"Sorry. I didn't mean—"

"I know," she interrupted. "I just, oh, never mind. We had a deal not to discuss anything too serious. How much longer until the sparkles?"

Not exactly how he recalled their "deal" conversation, but Caleb glanced at his watch. "About twenty minutes. Let's find a place to sit at Champ de Mars."

Maybe they could talk once there.

The park was decently lit. Mostly couples with a few families scattered over the grassy lawn. A few vendors went from group to group. They came to an area that wasn't too close to the others dreamily watching the tower.

"This looks like a good spot." Ivy moved her foot around over the grass.

"If I'd known we were going to do this, I would have brought a blanket." Or at least the lightweight jacket in his suitcase so that he could spread it for her to sit on.

"If I'd known we were going to do this, you wouldn't have had to," she countered, still riffling through the grass with her foot.

"Because you would have brought a blanket to sit on?" He hoped that's what she'd meant and that she wasn't implying that she'd have insisted upon being the one to stay at the hotel.

Nodding, then, facing the tower, she sat down. "I'm not worried about getting dirty, Caleb. This is a park. I just didn't want to have a smelly surprise if someone didn't clean up after their pet."

"Good thinking." He sat down next to her and might have gone for her hand, but she wrapped her arms around her knees and gazed up at the tower. The reflection lit her face, giving her an ethereal look. Beautiful.

Caleb grabbed his phone and snapped a shot.

Turning toward him, she arched a brow. "You missed. The tower is that way."

He shook his head. "I got what I wanted."

She breathed in sharply. "I think this place is getting to me."

"In what way?" Although, he knew. They were surrounded by amorous couples, and he longed for that blanket so they could lie back and stare up at the tower while cuddled together. *Cuddled?* Had he seriously just thought cuddled? He was not a cuddler. Not ever. Not even with Katrina when he'd been little more than a schoolkid.

"Being here makes me wonder at my life priorities," she answered after a few moments.

"Such as?"

"Actually, it's not really my life priorities that

are in question. At one time, I wanted a relationship, marriage, all those things, you know?"

"But you don't now?" he asked, glad she was
foregoing their not discussing anything serious.
They needed to discuss serious things. They'd be
on the flight home in the morning.

"I've been telling myself I don't ever since
Luke and I broke up."

Luke. The boyfriend who'd done her wrong.
The guy must have been an idiot to mess things
up with Ivy. "You said he cheated on you. What
happened?"

She hesitated, then blurted out, "He went
astray and blamed me."

"That's ballsy."

"I thought so at the time."

"You don't now?"

She propped her elbows against her knees and
stared at the tower. "Now I can't believe I'm wasting my breath talking about him, especially while
at one of the most romantic places in the world."

"With me."

"With you." Emotion gave her words a raspy
sound, hinting that being with him was as perti-
nent as where they were, perhaps more so.

"Can I hold your hand, Ivy?"

"You didn't ask a few minutes ago when we
were walking here," she reminded, eyeing him
curiously.

"True, but I feel as if I should ask now." Because his question was about much more than holding her hand and they both knew it. "Can I hold your hand, Ivy?"

She swallowed and for a moment, he wondered if she was going to reject him as she seemed to believe he'd done to her outside her room. But after a few moments, she shrugged.

"If you want to."

"I wouldn't have asked if I didn't want to, Ivy. The question is, do you want to hold my hand?"

Ivy wanted to. No doubt about that. Should she? was the real question. They would be heading home tomorrow, and everything would change. They'd no longer be caught up in the magic of France, but back in the real world. Nothing would be the same. Not between them and not in her life. She'd be sorting things at the farm, starting her job, and…missing moments like the one she was living.

"Yes, I'd like that."

"Me, too." Caleb took her hand, laced their fingers, and hand in hand, they tower-and-people-watched in silence. Again, it struck her how, despite everything, comfortable silence with Caleb was. She felt no need to say anything or to try to entertain him.

He glanced at his watch. "Less than a minute to go until the light show."

Never in a million years would Ivy have believed it if someone had told her two weeks ago she'd be sitting in a Parisian park with the most wonderful man she'd ever met, holding his hand even though he'd rejected her, and waiting for the Eiffel Tower to begin its show. Life sure could be strange.

The tower began to twinkle, sparkling in the sky.

"Oh! That's beautiful," Ivy breathed.

"Yes."

She glanced toward him. Around them couples were kissing and snapping photos. Ivy couldn't pull her gaze from his as the sparkling tower reflected in his amber eyes. "Caleb."

She didn't say anything more. Nothing more was needed. He knew everything she was thinking, feeling. He must have because he leaned toward her and, gaze locked with hers, pressed his lips to hers.

Ivy's stomach did flip-flops and somersaults and gymnastic moves worthy of a gold medal. Part of her longed to deepen the kiss, to throw her arms around him and push him back on the lawn and kiss him until neither of them could breathe. Another wanted to demand why he was kissing her when he'd walked away from her kisses just two nights ago. But there was something so magical about his gentle caressing of her mouth that she could only stare into his eyes and feel, completely mesmerized by what he was doing. By what was happening inside her chest. She was sparkling every bit as brightly as the tower. More so. Surely, she shined as bright a beacon over the city?

"Ville de l'Amour," a man said in a strong French accent from nearby, causing Ivy to jerk back from Caleb. How could she have forgotten that they were in a public park? Yes, there were lots of other couples, some of whom were still kissing, but Ivy had never been big on public displays of affection. Or maybe the men she'd dated had never been into PDA. She honestly wasn't sure.

"We should meet up with the others." She covered her mouth with her hand, as if that would somehow protect her from whatever it was Caleb's kiss had done to her. She certainly felt as if he'd cast a spell. Or maybe it was Paris. But whatever it was, it wasn't love. That's not what she was feeling. Friendship. Attraction. Euphoria from being in the most romantic city in the world. No wonder crazy things were happening inside her. That was the real allure of Paris. It made people long to believe in something that didn't seem to exist in her generation.

Ville de l'Amour, indeed. More like City of Make-Believe.

Their seating assignments were more scattered on the flight back to the States than they had been on their trip to France. Caleb had been assigned the aisle seat next to Owen and Suzie, but Slade asked to swap seats so he could sit beside Suzie. Caleb hadn't needed convincing. Slade's seat had been next to the woman whose kiss had added fireworks to the Eiffel Tower's light show the night before. No one might have seen the display, but Caleb had felt the explosions rock through him. Mini ones were going off while he currently held her hand.

No one could readily see their hands with how they were tucked low between them, but Ivy had held on tight when he'd taken her hand as the plane taxied down the runway for liftoff.

Glancing toward where Ivy hunkered into her seat, eyes closed, focusing on her breathing, he wished he could ease her fear of flying. "You okay, Doc?"

She lifted one lid enough to peek out at him. "I'm zooming through the air at five hundred miles an hour. What do you think?"

That she was beautiful, smart, funny and that he wished the plane would slow down so they'd have more time together. Two weeks with Ivy hadn't been nearly enough. Surely, she felt the same. How could she not after the kiss they'd shared the night before? He didn't consider himself a romantic man, but he couldn't imagine a more perfect kiss than sitting on the grassy lawn with the twinkling Eiffel Tower providing the mood lighting. Good grief, with thoughts like that, maybe he was a romantic man. Ivy made him feel romantic, made him want to be so he could shower her with affection and erase all traces of her exes' wrongs.

"I think you're doing great. Just keep focusing on your breathing. Deep breath in. Slow exhale out."

Her nostrils flared with another big breath in that she slowly blew out through pursed lips. "Yeah, it's not working. Distract me, Caleb," she ordered. "Tell me about you, something that I don't already know."

"Something you don't know?" He felt so connected to her it was difficult to imagine that there were still many things she didn't know about him. Yet, when those big blue eyes connected with his, he'd swear she knew him better than anyone in the ways that mattered most. "I grew up in Atlanta. My family still lives there."

"Atlanta's not too far from Knoxville. Just a few hours." They hit a bump of turbulence and she sucked in a few rapid deep breaths. "Keep talking."

Caleb gave her hand a reassuring squeeze. "I'm a middle child. My brother is older, and my sister is younger."

"You're lucky. I always wanted siblings. Tell me about them."

"They're both seemingly happily married and

have a couple of kids a piece, which is just another way I'm different."

Her gaze cut to him, and curiosity shone in her eyes.

"Not happily married and as far as I know, no kids," he continued, thinking her grasp had relaxed a little where she gripped his hand.

"How else are you different?"

"By worldly standards, they're very successful."

"And you're not?"

He'd never questioned his success while serving in the military, but what about since? He'd gone to school while rehabbing, was working to help Jordan, but did he see himself as successful when he no longer did what he longed to be doing?

"My life isn't what my parents would have chosen, but I'm content." He paused, then started over. "Actually, to say I've accepted my life would be more accurate than saying I'm content."

Had he really accepted that he would never jump again? His orthopedic surgeon assured him that jumping wasn't worth the risk and advised him not to do so. That Caleb had recovered too well to blow it on a moment's pleasure. Some days, he considered taking the chance just to feel the wind whipping around him again. Not as a paratrooper. He knew the army wouldn't take him back as a jumper with the hardware that remained in his leg, but just to jump for the exhilaration doing so gave him.

"I always knew I'd eventually have to do something after my paratrooper days, but I saw myself continuing in the army. I can reapply for enlistment, but my right tibia and fibula have plates and pins holding them together. They'd have to be removed first." Which his surgeon also did not recommend. "Even if I have surgery to remove my hardware, I'm in my thirties. That's older for a paratrooper, so if I opted to enlist, it would be to pursue a different military occupational specialty. I'd be starting from the ground up and have to requalify on all points."

Her eyes widened. "Are you considering enlisting again?"

"The army is never far from my thoughts. Going out on medical doesn't prevent me from reenlisting once healed. That doesn't mean they'd approve me again, though."

The plane shook with more turbulence and a noise sounded from deep in Ivy's throat.

"I've healed better than the orthopedic surgeon expected due to the amount of damage in my leg. I'm always aware of the injury, but it doesn't stop me from most aspects of my life."

"Did you land wrong? Is that how you fractured your leg?"

He hesitated long enough that she likely knew it had been more than a simple landing mishap.

He considered not telling her, but he wanted Ivy to know him the way he felt she already did. Things like how he'd gotten hurt were just life details to fill in the blanks of who he was.

"We jumped behind enemy lines, not knowing our mission had been compromised. Our plane was hit not long after we'd jumped. Shrapnel was all around us." The noise, smell and fear he'd felt in those moments flashed though his mind. "I was lucky that I was close to the ground when a piece of metal hit my leg."

Ivy's jaw dropped. "You could have been killed."

Blake had been. She'd wanted distraction. He'd achieved that because she looked at him with such intensity that, at least momentarily, she'd forgotten all about the plane.

"But I wasn't," he reminded. "My injured leg gave way upon impact with the ground, fracturing my leg bones in multiple areas." Was that pity in her eyes? He didn't need pity. Not from her or anyone. "I can do whatever I want except for high impact activities."

"Such as jumping out of an airplane?"

He snorted. "It's not the jumping that's the issue. It's the landing."

This time it was her giving his hand a squeeze. "Sorry, not sorry."

His brow arched.

"The thought of you jumping out of an airplane terrifies me," she admitted.

Yet he longed to experience that rush. "It's the greatest, most peaceful feeling in the world when you're up there."

"We'll just have to disagree, because I can assure you 'a peaceful feeling' is not what I'd be experiencing if I was free-falling through the sky."

He half smiled. "Maybe not, but for me, there's nothing better than when I'm up there."

He attempted to explain the beauty of the earth below, the intense colors of the atmosphere, the way he connected with every breath and beat of his body and how everything came into focus. Ivy listened to his words, hearing the passion in his voice, hearing the grief in how much he obviously missed something he'd loved so much. But no amount of words was going to convince her to jump out of a plane.

"How did you end up a paramedic?" she asked. "Did it have something to do with your care after your leg injury?"

"That would make sense under normal circumstances, but I was in the Middle East. The only help coming for me was my brothers-and-sisters-in-arms. So my accident wasn't how it happened. Not really, although it indirectly played a role," he admitted. "I was in a bad mental place after my injury. I was pushing my body as far as I could with my physical therapy, but my mind had too much free time to dwell on the things that had happened. It wasn't good. I wasn't good. An army buddy convinced me to go back to school so I could work at TransCare. It was a turning point for me. I owe Jordan a lot."

"I've seen TransCare advertisements."

"Probably the billboard on I-40."

"That's right. I have seen that. If your friend was smart, he'd put your photo on that ad. You'd be getting all kinds of calls."

Caleb chuckled. "Jordan's a she and I'll be sure to tell her."

Surprise shone in Ivy's eyes. "Your army buddy is a woman?"

"Yep. There are women paratroopers. We met in airborne school. I had planned to be a lifer, but that was never her intention. She always talked about how much she loved Knoxville and, as much as she loved jumping, she didn't reenlist, but went to paramedic school instead."

"And convinced you to do the same."

"As I said, I was in a bad mental place when she convinced me that she needed my help. I'm not sure she really did. She's tough and would have made it without me, but as my buddy Blake's widow, I'd do anything for her, and she knew it."

Ivy had a million questions, but hadn't she already decided that she and Caleb were just a fairy tale of their circumstances? They'd been thrown together for two weeks in the most romantic country in the world. No wonder they'd gotten caught up in the fairy tale. Who wouldn't have?

Soon they'd be home and back to the real world. Caleb Rivers wouldn't look so wonderfully perfect then. Besides, did she really think he was any different from every other man who'd interested her? That her making more than him wouldn't eventually get to him and undermine how he viewed and treated her? But what if she was wrong?

"Do you see yourself working for TransCare long term, then?"

He considered a moment, then shrugged. "I'm not sure. I'd reenlist if I could jump, but that isn't in my future. I enjoy working at TransCare, plus I owe it to Blake to help Jordan for however long she needs me, so who knows? I might stay there."

"What about money?" What an awkward conversation? "Do you make enough to get by okay on your paramedic pay?"

"I get by. My wants are pretty basic." He eyed her curiously. "What about you? Are you going to get by okay or are you bogged down with student loans from med school?"

She was botching this but didn't know better words to use than just asking him forthright. "Does it bother you that I make more money than you?"

His forehead scrunched. "Should it?"

"I…" She thought over Luke's cruel words, his accusation that she'd made him feel inferior. She couldn't imagine Caleb ever feeling inferior. But in the beginning, would she have thought Luke would? He'd had a good job, was successful at what he did and had seemed secure in who he was. That he'd eventually felt the need to berate her at every opportunity, had her saying, "Yeah, I think it should."

What was she doing? He'd not said he wanted a relationship with her. Not really. Yes, she saw it in his eyes, but the past haunted her. She just didn't think she could take Caleb breaking her heart. Much better to be up-front and give voice to her concerns.

He let go of her hand, twisted in his seat to more fully face her. "It doesn't, but that you think it should, does bother me. Care to explain?"

"It's not that it bothers me. It's that it's going to bother you that you aren't more…" That didn't come out right, because, really, could she imagine him being more than what he was when he seemed close to perfect? But she couldn't take back her poor word choice, couldn't erase how his face splotched red.

"That I'm not more than who I am?" His jaw tightened. "You mean financially?"

Ivy inwardly cringed. This conversation felt so wrong. It was wrong. They were sitting on a plane over the Atlantic Ocean and she was grilling Caleb over the mistakes she'd made in choosing past relationships.

"After my breakup with Luke, I promised myself that I wasn't going to become involved with anyone who didn't make more money than me. Then, I met you and you seem so wonderful, but be honest, the past two weeks have been anything but reality. Relationships are difficult enough without disproportionate incomes creating feelings of insecurity. I've been through that three times, and each time it's ended with my heart getting trampled on."

"I'm not your ex."

"I know that, but what about down the road? Relationships always seem shiny in the beginning, but eventually a person needs to learn to keep her eyes open to what's coming." Was she trying to convince him or herself?

He eyed her a minute then shook his head. "So, basically you don't want a relationship with me because I don't make more money than you?" Disappointment shone on his handsome face. "There are things far more important about a person than what's written on their bank statement. I didn't think that was who you were, Ivy, that a job title or bank account mattered so much to you."

How did she explain that she knew it would matter to *him* at some future point? That the past had taught her that eventually his masculinity would feel threatened, and he'd take it out on her? Caleb feeling threatened by anything seemed impossible, but she refused to be made a fool of again.

"The past two weeks have been wonderful, Caleb." Taking a deep breath, she said what she believed needed to be said. For both of them. Better to end things now than to feel the complete devastation that would come if she and Caleb embarked on a relationship, and he betrayed her. How would she ever recover from *him*? "A trip I've dreamed of in so many ways, but I never intended to meet someone. I have a lot going on in my life and you don't fit in with those plans."

Was that disgust in his eyes? Or just a reflection of what she was feeling bouncing back at her? Her words made her stomach roil. No matter. If she didn't completely end things with Caleb, he might convince her to give their relationship a go and then when things fell apart, she'd be utterly devastated. She might not have known him long, but she recognized that Caleb was different, that her reactions to him were more potent, that he had more power over her than any man ever had and that scared her. Much better to remember France as the magical experience it was than to sully the memory with a tragic ending to the fairy tale.

CHAPTER ELEVEN

"You're invited to join Roy at his A Century of Life celebration." Ivy read out the card and smiled. She'd gone to the last Smoky Mountain Veteran Foundation monthly meeting. Being with the group had filled her with such mixed emotions. Happiness at seeing the people she felt so close with. Glad that Caleb wasn't there. Glad? That wasn't the only emotion she'd felt. Not by far. She missed him.

Had she secretly been hoping he would be? Apparently, he and Stan had volunteered with a fundraiser a few weeks prior. Ivy had been scheduled in the emergency department that Saturday and hadn't been able to attend. When she'd heard that he'd been there, she'd felt…longing. How could she miss someone she'd only spent two weeks with?

Other than the fact that she couldn't seem to keep him from her mind, she'd fallen into a good routine over the past two months, working at the farm to sort through her grandfather's paperwork and business affairs. Fortunately, Mr. Griggs wanted to continue leasing the land for his cattle and crops, lifting a huge burden off Ivy for at least the next few years. Her hospital work crew was awesome and she'd already made several friends whom she adored. Life was good.

Only, it wasn't.

There was a huge hole in her chest the size of which she'd never known. Yes, she grieved Gramps and always would, but she'd come to terms with his death, knowing he'd lived a good life, and that he'd known how much she adored him. She'd miss him always. But it was Caleb she missed in ways that made no sense. Then again, how many dates did one have to go on to equal being together almost nonstop for two weeks?

He'd never been to the farm, so why could she look around the kitchen and see him standing at the sink? Or walk to the pond and see him sitting on the bank, fishing pole in hand, trying to catch one of the many fish her grandfather had stocked it with years before? Why, when she closed her eyes, did she transport from a grassy park at the base of the Eiffel Tower to lying on a blanket in a field with him with the Smoky Mountains as their backdrop?

Would he be at Roy's party? Outside of her imaginings, she'd not seen him. Not that he hadn't been at the hospital. He had. There was always an excited buzz from the single female hospital staff anytime he was in the building. One bolder nurse said she'd given him her phone number.

Oh, how that would hurt, to see or hear of Caleb with another woman. She'd experienced it before. Kenny had almost immediately started dating other girls when Ivy had left for college. Beau had gotten his ex-girlfriend pregnant while he and Ivy were still dating. Luke had cheated on her with the college student and looking back, that probably wasn't his first time cheating, just the first she'd caught him. And, although Ivy had been heartbroken, she wasn't so sure it had been over the man so much as the betrayal. Three times and she was out. It was what she'd told herself prior to her trip to France.

One of the cardiologists had asked her out a few times, but Ivy hadn't gone, telling him she had no interest in dating. He met the dating conditions she'd set, was a nice guy, but it was the truth. She didn't want to date. How could she when she missed a man whom she'd spent two fantastic weeks with more than she'd thought possible.

Going to her bedroom, she opened her nightstand drawer and pulled out the postcard of the church he'd given her. Nostalgia hit, as did tears, and soon she was sobbing as intensely as she had while sitting on the bloodstained pew. Only, this time, Caleb wasn't there to hold her while she cried. No one was.

Reaching for her cellphone, she dialed a number. "Mom, is my trunk still in my old room's closet? Yes? Awesome. Is it okay if I come to Nashville? I'd like to have it and spend some time with you and Dad."

"Happy birthday to you. Happy birthday, dear Roy. Happy birthday to you! And many more!" Cheers erupted in the Strawberry Plains church community room where Roy's birthday party was being held. Roy had lived in the east Tennessee town most of his life and there was a large crowd of friends and family, including many from the SMVF.

"Can you believe our whole group from Normandy made it today for Dad's party?" Mary enthused, handing Ivy a cup of punch. "I can't begin to convey how happy that makes me. Dad and I talk about how close we felt to everyone there and how much we've missed seeing everyone together the past three months."

Ivy knew exactly how Mary felt. She experienced it herself.

"Would you look at Slade and Suzie?" Mary beamed at the young couple. "They're as cute as can be and still making googly eyes at each other."

Ivy glanced toward them, and they did look very much in love as they chatted with Linda and her husband. Owen was with them, as was Paul.

"But I will admit that I'm disappointed about one thing," Mary continued, causing Ivy's gaze to shift back to her. "I am stunned that you and Caleb dropped the ball on what was happening between you in France."

Ivy inwardly cringed. She had enough second guesses without Mary adding to them. So she took a sip of punch then smiled at the lady she'd come to adore. "France was a magical place and made things seem shinier than what they were, Mary. That's all."

Mary's red-brown brow arched. "Do you believe that?"

Ivy sought out where Caleb stood, fruit punch in hand, talking with Jimmy. As if sensing she was looking his way, his amber eyes shifted to where they stared directly into hers. Then, just as quickly, he looked away, dousing her with ice water.

Ivy swallowed the lump that formed in her throat, but still could barely breathe. She'd not been able to stop thinking about him. The shine hadn't worn off. Not for her. For Caleb, he couldn't even stand to look at her. Nausea tightened her throat.

What had she done?

"France wasn't what made certain things appear shiny," Mary unnecessarily pointed out. "A person only had to look at you two together to see the sparks."

"It doesn't matter now, Mary." She'd been too scared of failure, of getting hurt, to even try with Caleb. What was it about relationships that always had her making the wrong decisions? "It's too late to go back to the way things were."

"What do you mean, go back to the way things were? You don't need to go back. You need to go forward, working through whatever it is that kept you two from the kind of happiness that Slade and Suzie have found in each other."

Ivy's knees wobbled, and she moved to a nearby chair. "I'm not sure going forward is a possibility."

Mary sat down in the chair next to her. "You disappoint me. I didn't think of you as someone who was afraid to love."

"I'm not." She'd loved Gramps with all her heart. She loved her parents, even if they were very different from herself. She'd seen them twice over the past month, once when she'd gone to Nashville, and again when they'd visited the farm. Her mother had admitted that she'd felt Gramps and Grammie had resented her for being born because their only child had died giving birth to her. Ivy wasn't so sure they hadn't. But whatever the disconnect between her mother and great-grandparents, they'd all loved her. And she'd loved them. She wasn't afraid to love.

She'd loved Kenny in the way one loves their high school sweetheart. She'd loved Beau in the way that one loves the guy they date through their undergrad. And she'd loved Luke in that way one loved someone they date through residency. But she'd not been in love with any of them. Not a one.

Her gaze shifted to Caleb and she bit into her lower lip. She didn't love him. She couldn't.

"Maybe I *am* afraid to love." Her eyes stung. Her lungs ached. Maybe she'd been afraid all along and that was why she'd clung to her stupid "condition" to not date anyone who didn't earn more than her. It had never been about the condition, but about how she feared making herself vulnerable to someone. Because that's what she hadn't done before, what had made the real disparity in those relationships. She'd never let anyone in, never put them on equal ground to guard her heart and best interests.

Mary stared at her a moment, then shook her head. "Then you don't deserve him."

"You're right. I didn't." Question was, could she change that? Could she prove to him that she could love, and could he ever love her in return?

With a busy crowd of birthday guests, Caleb hadn't had too much difficulty in avoiding Ivy. At least not until she had specifically sought him out. Which he found surprising after the way she'd decimated him on the plane.

"I wanted to thank you for my postcard." Looking at him a bit nervously, she smiled. "I brought my souvenir trunk home." She half smiled. "My parents were shocked that I wanted my trunk."

"What made you after all this time?"

"You."

"Glad I could be of assistance on something." Ivy was full of surprises. Surprises he didn't need to hear. The past three months hadn't been great for him. He could have easily slipped into places he never wanted to return to. "If you'll excuse me, I'm going to go tell Roy happy birthday one last time, then head home."

He turned to walk away but her words stayed him.

"I miss you."

He sucked in a deep breath. "I can't do this, Ivy."

She glanced around the crowded room. "You're right. This isn't the time or place to talk about us."

He shook his head. "There is no us."

She'd ended any possibility of that on the plane.

She winced. "I… Will you come to the farm, Caleb?"

He stared at her, wondering what it was about her that got to him so much. He'd been wondering for three months and come up with a thousand answers. Her eyes. Her smile. Her laugh. Her intelligence. Her passion. The way she'd loved her great-grandfather. The list went on. There were just as many reasons for him not to go to her farm. Reasons that included two weeks in France that had forever changed him.

Perhaps she sensed that he was about to refuse, because she touched his arm, shooting awareness through him just the same as her touch had from the beginning. "Please. There are things I need to say. If you don't want to hear them, then I understand, but if I ever meant anything to you, then please do this for me."

If she'd ever meant anything to him? That was almost comical. Just two weeks ago, he'd had lunch with Josh, and stunned himself and his brother by asking about the company. He'd quickly relented, knowing he didn't want to work for the shipping company. But for a moment, he'd considered. Because he'd wanted to do something to impress Ivy, to prove to her that he was worthy. He was worthy. He didn't need a title or to work for a big company to prove that. That he'd even for a second considered it because of the woman standing before him was enough that he should run. She made him want to do whatever it took to win her heart.

But if she couldn't love him for who he was, then she didn't really love him.

"What did you have in mind?" Because he always had lived on the edge. Why stop now?

Her gaze searched his and she gave him a hopeful look. "What are you doing right now?"

"I have plans." When he'd told Jordan about his

mental lapse with his brother, she'd made him an offer that he might not be able to refuse. And that might, eventually, impress the woman standing before him. Not that Ivy was why he was meeting with Jordan or likely to take up her offer.

"Oh." Ivy's face fell. "I…okay. I understand. When are you available?"

Caleb ran his fingers through his hair, then glanced around the room. Roy and Owen were watching them and simultaneously gave a thumbs-up. Mary, too. Caleb sighed. "Text me your address. I'll message you when I'm free."

Ivy glanced around her home, wondering how it would look through Caleb's eyes. She'd not made any major changes to the decor, but had hired a contractor to have walls painted, the kitchen modernized, a few other odds and ends around the place that needed done. She'd been slowly going through things, deciding what she wanted to keep, and what she wanted to replace with items that were more her style as she made the farmhouse truly into her home.

She worried that having Caleb inside the house meant she'd never be able to erase the images of him having been there. Already he haunted everywhere she looked. Because no matter where she went, what she did, he was there. In her heart. Which she was about to completely expose to Caleb. She didn't expect him to easily forgive her, but she prayed he'd at least hear her out and give her a second chance to prove to him that, through her eyes, he was perfect just as he was. Perfect for her.

If he didn't give her that chance, well, she'd wish him well and die a little inside. A lot inside.

A knock sounded at the front door. Ivy sucked in a deep breath. Too late for doubts. He was here. Thank God, because part of her had wondered if he'd text that he had changed his mind.

Oh, God. He'd liked her. Although he'd gone back to his room that night at Phillipe and Delphine's, he had liked her. On that plane, he'd not looked at her with "like." Far from it. What had she done, pushing him away because of her own silly insecurities? Had she really let Luke's digs punch such holes in her belief in her worthiness to be loved that she'd pushed away a man who'd stolen her heart and might have grown to love her someday?

She opened the door, damping down the butterflies in her stomach that Caleb was at the farm and about to enter her home. He still wore his jeans and TransCare T-shirt and looked so gorgeous she could barely breathe. "You came."

He took his sunglasses off and slipped an earpiece over his T-shirt collar. "I told you I would."

He was a man of his word. She knew that about him. Caleb was honorable and lived by a code she'd admired for so long. It was a remnant from a dying generation. He was whom she'd been waiting to meet her entire life, whom every day of her life had been preparing her for, and she'd been too blind to realize it.

She gulped back the ball of emotions clogging her throat.

Get it together, Ivy. He's here. That has to mean something. Maybe not as much as you want it to mean, but it's a start.

"I thought we could sit on the back porch. I have lemonade made."

"Lemonade?" He raked his hand over his jaw. "This isn't really a social call, Ivy. Tell me what you wanted me to come out here for and let's get this over with."

He didn't want to be here. That code of honor she'd just acknowledged demanded that he give her the opportunity to say her piece, but he didn't want her under the false impression that he wanted to be there. He obviously didn't.

"I— Okay, then, I'll get right to it." Part of her just wanted to forget all the things she'd been mulling over, trying to figure out how to say how wrong she'd been. But Mary's words haunted her. If she wasn't strong enough to risk her heart, she didn't deserve Caleb. Mary was right. Baring one's heart wasn't easy after a lifetime of never sharing it. "I have missed you more than I would have believed possible of someone I spent two weeks with."

Caleb's jaw tightened. Ivy rushed on because she wasn't weak. She wasn't content with being the product of Luke's derogatory remarks. She was the granddaughter of a brave WWII paratrooper and she wanted this man standing before her. More than wanted him.

"I told myself that what I felt for you was because of where we were, because we were away from reality in this idyllic place that was in many ways a fantasy for me. I even tried to tell myself that my grief over Gramps played a role in my emotions latching on to you. And maybe all of those things did set the background for what was happening, but the reality is, no matter where I met you, no matter what the circumstances, no matter how long we had together, my heart still would have chosen you."

Caleb couldn't believe what Ivy was saying. The entire drive to her place he'd run a dozen scenarios through his mind of what she wanted to say. He'd settled on her wanting to apologize, maybe be friends.

"What happened to you not dating anyone who wasn't your financial equal?" Technically, she hadn't said she wanted to date him. But surely saying her heart would have chosen him implied that she wanted to date him?

Looking repentant, she took a deep breath. "That stipulation was my safeguard after Luke's betrayal. I told myself that if I eliminated that issue then I didn't have to worry about a repeat happening. But deep down I knew Luke's cheating wasn't because of the disparity in our incomes, but because I never trusted him with my heart. He cheated because he wasn't the man he should have been. He didn't have the honor he should have had. Gramps was never crazy about him, you know?"

Feeling as if he needed to do something with his hands, Caleb hooked his thumbs into his jeans' belt loopholes. "I can't imagine he'd like someone who cheated on you."

"Gramps never knew. Thank God or there's no telling what he would have done. I might have had to bail him out of jail. He'd have seen it as his duty to defend my honor."

Caleb imagined if he ever had a daughter or granddaughter that he'd feel the same.

"He'd have liked you."

His gaze met hers. "You think?"

"I know. You're all the things he found important in a person."

"You spent two weeks with me, Ivy," he reminded. "You barely know me."

What she had known hadn't been enough. She'd wanted him to be more, to have more. She'd said that had just been an excuse, but she'd echoed Katrina's words and that couldn't be a coincidence.

"Do you really believe that?" Ivy shook her head, then reached out, taking her hands into his. "Because I don't. Oh, I may not know all the details of your life, but I know you, Caleb. The man you are inside, the things that make you tick. I know you're honorable, kind, generous, loyal, determined, strong and exactly the man I need in my life just as you are."

He was stunned. Completely and totally stunned by what Ivy was saying. He sucked air in, then slowly blew it out. "Well, that may be a problem because I just committed to a major change in my life."

Her head spun. She'd laid out her heart, and deep down, she believed Caleb cared about her. He wouldn't be here if he didn't. But his tone was foreboding. What kind of commitment had he made prior to arriving at her house?

"What kind of commitment?"

"A couple of weeks ago, Jordan asked me to be her partner at TransCare."

"That's great." Then worrying that he'd think she would think that because of the things she'd said on the plane, she started over. "I mean, if that's what you want. Is it?"

He nodded. "I think so. When TransCare was first getting started, she offered to make me a partner if I'd help her with the business. I thought she was just trying to pull me out of where I was and there's likely some truth to that, but she was serious."

"That's wonderful, Caleb. I'm happy for you."

"I'm going to be busy over the next few months as I transition into taking on more responsibilities." Was he trying to tell her that he wouldn't have time for whatever she had in mind? Or was he spitting her own words back at her that she'd used on him on the plane?

"Too busy to share dinner with me from time to time?"

He hesitated, seeming to consider. "As your friend?"

"My friend. My lover. My everything." There. She'd dropped all barriers and exposed her poor heart.

He stared at her, not saying anything.

"Caleb?" Her heart thundered in her chest. "I… I basically just told you that I love you. Please say something."

"You love me?"

She gulped back the fears assailing her that she couldn't read his face. "With all my heart. I'm so sorry for the things I said on the plane, Caleb. I didn't want to make another relationship mistake. It took being away from you for me to realize that, no matter what happens in the future, not giving us a chance is the biggest mistake I could ever make." She gave his hands a gentle squeeze. "There's nothing you need to prove. There never was. I was just too blinded by fear of exposing my heart." She stared straight into his eyes, emphasizing each word of her next sentence. "You are worth everything."

Slowly a smile spread across his face. "Everything?"

"Everything that matters." Her hands shook. "Honestly, nothing seems to matter much without you, Caleb. I've missed you so much."

"The feeling is mutual, Ivy."

"Then you forgive me?"

He lifted her hands to his lips and pressed a kiss there. "Always."

"Always should work out just about perfect. Because that's how long I'm going to want you in my life, Caleb. Always."

His gaze locked with hers and she'd swear they were watery with emotion as he said, "Show me."

Ivy did, giving him her heart and having his. Then and for always.

EPILOGUE

"You doing okay over there?"

Eyes tightly closed, Ivy squeezed the edges of her plane seat. "You're distracting me, Caleb. Don't talk."

From where he sat beside her in the aisle seat, Caleb chuckled. "I distinctly recall you asking me to distract you the last time we were in a plane together."

"That was my way of getting you to tell me all your secrets," she admitted, still not opening her eyes.

"And now that you know everything there is to know about me, you want me to keep quiet?" He sounded amused.

"Do I know all of your secrets?" She opened her eyes long enough to glance his way.

"All that matter."

"I guess you're going to have to come up with a new way of distracting me during flights, then." Not that she'd learned everything there was to know about him over the past nine months. She was sure she hadn't, but he had proven her right to give him her heart. Caleb made her feel treasured, and just as he'd done while in France, when he spoke to her, of her, it was with praise and admiration. With love. She glanced at him, filled with how much she adored him. "I can't believe I let you talk me into this."

"If I recall correctly, you were the one who said we couldn't tell the foundation no when they asked us to head up the medical team again this year."

"We couldn't," she admitted, glancing around to visually check on their veterans who were within her line of vision. "I was just in denial about how we'd have to get to France. Too bad we can't drive."

"Across the Atlantic?" He arched his brow at her. "No thanks."

"Okay, you're right." She took a deep breath, then admitted, "It will be nice to see Phillipe and Delphine. It was so nice of them to agree to host us again. You think they'll give us our old rooms?"

A noise crackled over the PA system, then a stewardess announced, "Are there any medical personnel on the plane? Would any medical personnel on the plane please come to the back galley."

Ivy gasped, her gaze going to Caleb's. "I can't believe this is happening again."

"What is it with you and planes?" he said, undoing his seat belt. He was already halfway to the back of the plane by the time Ivy had her seat belt unfastened and her backpack slid out from beneath the seat. This time she was bringing her bag with her from the get-go, so they'd hopefully have whatever they needed close.

Only, when she rounded the corner of the galley Mary and several of the stewardess huddled around Caleb, but Ivy didn't see a distressed passenger.

Confused, Ivy glanced around, looking for whoever needed medical help. "What's going on? Is there an emergency?"

Suddenly she registered that Mary and one of the stewardesses held phones, recording what was happening. Her eyes widened. Her heart pounded. She could barely breathe. Her fingers flew to her mouth, covering the cry she emitted. Over the past several months they'd shared so many dreams, including hopes for their future, but she hadn't been expecting this, not yet. Not *here*.

"Ivy McEwen, one year ago, we were on a flight to Paris, and you saved a woman's life. Everyone knew that. What most didn't realize was that you also saved mine. After my injury, I thought the best parts of my life were over, but I was wrong." He took her hand into his and kissed her fingertips. "The best parts were just beginning with meeting you."

Ivy's hand shook. Her entire body shook. Was this really happening or had she fallen asleep over the Atlantic? Or maybe the plane had gone down and she was in heaven?

Caleb knelt on one knee and Ivy's legs wobbled.

"Ivy, I've been thinking about how I wanted to do this for a long time. On a plane seemed the obvious choice."

"Obviously," she mumbled, still stunned by what he was doing and by the sparkly diamond and ruby ring he'd pulled from his pocket.

"I've never known anyone like you, Ivy. I know that's because you are one of a kind. Your uniqueness just adds to your charm, and you've certainly charmed me from the moment we met. Will you marry me, Ivy?"

Placing her hands upon his cheeks, she lowered to her knees because she didn't feel capable of standing a moment longer. "Yes, Caleb. Even on a plane, which you know I hate, my answer is yes!"

His amber eyes looking glassy, he smiled, slid the ring onto her finger, then laced their hands. "I love you, Ivy. With everything I am I will love you forever and protect you and any children we may have."

Happiness bursting from her, she nodded. "I love you right back, Caleb. Now and forever and any future babies we have." She thought a moment, then told him, "I'm going to want a boy to name after Gramps."

"I'd be proud for our son to have your great-grandfather's name. And if we have a girl, we'll just keep trying until we have a boy." Caleb kissed her. A deep kiss that had her thinking the plane was plummeting as she held on to him.

Clapping and cheers sounded around them from those in the galley.

Caleb stood, then helped her to her feet only to lift her and spin her around. "You make me feel like the luckiest man alive."

"Good, because you just made me the luckiest woman alive."

Ivy hugged Mary, showed her ring off proudly, then eventually, hand clasped with Caleb's, made her way back to their seats. They'd made it about halfway there when the PA system came back on. "Ladies and gentlemen, the stewardess informs me that congratulations are in order. She said yes."

The passengers erupted into clapping. Ivy's face went hot, but she smiled and thanked everyone before sliding into her seat.

When they were settled and their seat belts refastened, she shook her head at Caleb. "You've done it now."

He grinned. "What?"

"Completely set the bar high for distracting me while flying. How will you ever top this?"

Laughing, he leaned forward and kissed the corner of her mouth. "I have the rest of our lives. I'll think of something."

And he did.

* * * * *

If you enjoyed this story, check out these other great reads from Janice Lynn

Breaking the Nurse's No-Dating Rule
Heart Doctor's Summer Reunion
The Single Mom He Can't Resist
Reunited with the Heart Surgeon

All available now!